Cover art by:
Daniela Owergoor
http://dani-owergoor.deviantart.com/

Happy New Year
(The Time Bubble Book 10)

By Jason Ayres

For Laura

Contents

Chapter One
2016

I've really grown to hate New Year. What do I hate so much about it? Pretty much everything, if I'm honest, and that was even before I got stuck in this time loop. Now I'm living every depressing detail of each and every one of them all over again.

Where do I start? Well, the biggest problem is that it's my birthday. I was born on 1st January 1986 which makes me thirty-nine years old, or at least I was before all this time-travelling business started. People say I look younger – men mostly who are trying to get me into bed. That isn't meant to sound bitter. It's just the voice of experience from one who's been there, done it, and bought and thrown away the T-shirt as far as men are concerned – or one man in particular, if truth be told, but more about him later.

If I am being brutally honest, and hopefully reasonably modest, until recently when I looked in the mirror I would say I could pass for thirty-five. That's not first thing in the morning, obviously, but no one looks great at that time of day unless they're in a movie waking up after a night of improbably romantic sex.

I'm talking at least an hour after I've woken up, when I've washed, moisturised and had two cups of coffee to make me feel human again. Oh, and I've done my hair. Unlike those Hollywood starlets, I don't have my own personal stylist to make my hair look perfect while I'm asleep.

Despite its bedraggled early morning look, my best feature probably is my hair. It's long, blonde and without a hint of grey in sight. Before she died, I remember my mother telling me the grey hairs will start showing up when I hit forty. With all that's been happening to me lately, I'm not sure I will ever reach that milestone.

You see, I don't have to pass for being thirty-five anymore because, as of today, I'm only thirty. In two days' time, I'll turn twenty-nine. Confused yet? I sure as hell was when all this started happening. That was about three weeks ago, since when it's been permanently New Year – which, you'll recall, is not my favourite time of year.

1st January must be a strong contender for the worst possible date on which to have a birthday. Only 25th December could trump it. There was a girl I went to school with in Liverpool who was born on Christmas Day. Siobhan had really mean grandparents who always bought her a joint birthday and Christmas present which was a pretty flimsy excuse for getting away with buying just one. It wasn't as if they even spent twice the money – she would get a cheap Tamagotchi off the Heritage Market at Stanley Dock if she was lucky.

I didn't mind being born on 1st January when I was still a child. Apparently, everyone made a real fuss of me when I was born because I was the first baby born at the Liverpool Women's Hospital in 1986. I was supposed to have been born the previous day but clung onto my mother's womb until twelve minutes after midnight. Being the first meant I even got my picture in *The Echo*. It was my first and last moment of fame – I've not appeared in a newspaper since.

As I grew up, being born on the 1st of January still seemed like a good thing. I never had to go to school on my birthday and because it was a bank holiday there were always plenty of family members around to celebrate.

Some years we would go and visit my maternal grandparents in Oxford. On others, they would come and stay with us. These were my happiest years, before my mum and dad split. After that I started being dragged from one end of the country to the other, losing some of my sense of identity in the process.

From that point, my birthday celebrations took a nosedive. By the time I hit my late-teens and early twenties and wanted to go out drinking and partying to celebrate my birthday, nobody was interested. They were always too hung-over from the night before.

"I can't see what the problem is," said Kelly, who was my best friend at the time. "I think you're lucky. The whole country goes out to celebrate your birthday." That was on my 21st.

Blatantly they didn't but I couldn't be bothered to point out the flaws in that argument so just went along with it. I knew that my friends weren't really celebrating my birthday, even if they could be bothered to pretend they were. They, like everyone else, were out to enjoy New Year's Eve.

It was only when Big Ben chimed that my birthday celebrations could truly begin and, invariably, they didn't. Everyone around always wished me "Happy New Year" but hardly anyone ever said, "Happy Birthday". In their drunken euphoria, they had forgotten all about me. Going out to celebrate my birthday? I think not.

"Let's go out for lunch on my actual birthday, tomorrow," I suggested one year, not long before Big Ben chimed. Of course, everyone was up for it in their drunken state. The following lunchtime I sat like a total numpty in Nando's like some Billy-no-mates, realisation slowly dawning that no one was going to turn up. Not one of them even bothered to text. Most were probably still in bed. Even an extra-large dollop of peri-peri sauce couldn't sate my disappointment.

After I turned thirty, birthdays became less of a big deal. I felt less inclined to go out and get drunk every year than I had before. I was working full-time as a nurse by then and the enhanced pay for working over the bank holiday period was well worth missing yet another tedious New Year's Eve party for. It was enough to pay for a nice week away in the Canaries in January just as everyone else was struggling back to work.

I loved going on holiday at that time of year. It was cheap as chips outside the school holidays. I felt sorry for people with kids when I looked at the astronomical prices travel agents charged during the school holidays. How did they ever afford to get away?

I was determined to make the most of the years before I had children to travel as much as possible, but to be honest, a week each year in Lanzarote wasn't exactly travelling the world as I had in my younger years.

I would go with Rob, my ex, and we always got on better when we were away. In the latter years, it was about the only time we communicated at all, but as I later discovered, he had other distractions back home.

I didn't work every New Year. Of those I did not, I could honestly say I had only had one decent birthday in the past decade. That was last year when my two eager young flatmates pushed the boat out and made the effort for me. Prior to that, virtually every other birthday in my thirties had been a non-event.

Rob, whom I lived with for several years, never seemed bothered about me working during the holiday period. Since he was shagging the girl next door behind my back for at least half the time we were living together, I guess he saw it as an opportunity for a little extra-curricular activity. It was actually on my birthday four years ago when he dropped the bombshell he was leaving me for her.

You might be thinking that was rather heartless. Could he not at least have waited until the day after? Actually, he couldn't, as it was on that particular day I caught the pair of

4

them in bed together. Would he ever have told me if I hadn't stumbled on them as I had? Would I have lived with him another four years in blissful ignorance?

I only found out then after coming home early from work because I was poorly. Yes, I had a terrible cold as well, just one more thing to make the misery of that day complete. It was definitely one of my all-time worst New Years, and I've had some shockers, believe me.

Aside from my own personal issues, there's one other thing I really detest about New Year and that is all the false hope and bravado that people come out with.

"This year's going to be my year," they say.

"It's time for a fresh start," they proclaim.

Then they carry right on making all the same mistakes they did the previous year, whilst unrealistically expecting different results. You would think they would learn from experience but most never do. So it's the same dead-end jobs, the same bad boyfriends, the same drink, drugs and bad food.

It's annoying enough when they go on about it to your face but it's even worse when it's plastered all over Facebook. Some seem to regurgitate almost word for word the same rubbish they spouted the previous year – and the year before that. I don't know why they don't just cut and paste it and be done with it.

Some of them boldly declare their resolutions, but what's the point? They never keep them. And why tell all and sundry via social media? They are only setting themselves up to look foolish and weak-willed when it all goes pear-shaped.

There's one girl that I used to work with who has a long history of choosing inappropriate men – basically, she is addicted to bad boys. When they crap all over her all we hear is "all men are bastards" and get the big victim act. A couple of weeks later it all goes quiet as she starts screwing the next one – who of course is a carbon copy of the previous one. But none of this is her fault, of course.

Last New Year she pronounced on Facebook that she was finished with men for good. Last I heard she was pregnant by a guy she met in February who has kids by four different women and has since been done for GBH.

Another friend and current colleague claims to be a size eighteen but is actually nearer twenty-six. She starts Weight Watchers every January and wow, do we get to hear about it – constantly. We get daily updates for a few weeks of how well she's doing and then it all goes strangely quiet. This is around the time the lure of the cream cakes becomes too much.

This resolution/fresh start stuff is just complete bollocks. Forlorn hopes, shallow promises, the whole thing is just so forced and false. 2nd January is probably my favourite day of the year due to the relief of it being all over.

The first thing I do on that day is get the Christmas tree down and remove all evidence of the festivities from the house. My flatmates sometimes complain that it's bad luck but I can't understand people who keep that stuff up until Twelfth Night. Who honestly still feels Christmassy looking at tinsel and lights on the 5th of January?

Once it's all gone my home looks refreshingly bare, and normality can resume. Or at least that used to be the case because, for me, normality no longer exists. It seems that I'm stuck permanently with New Year for the rest of my life, which by my calculations is not long. As things currently stand it looks like I've got a life expectancy of about two months.

I guess it's high time I explained what the hell I'm talking about. Well, it kind of goes like this…

Chapter Two
2025

When it first happened, I was confused to begin with, almost amnesiac. But now I can recall in great detail everything that occurred on *that day*.

After the initial period of disorientation and shock my mind cleared and I've now been over the events that occurred hundreds of times. I thought if I analysed it in that much detail I might eventually pick up some clue that might help me form a plan to get me out of this predicament. So far I've drawn a blank.

It was 1st January 2025, just another bog-standard New Year's Day. There was nothing remarkable about it other than it being my birthday and you already know how I feel about that. It was a particularly significant birthday for me, but before you ask, it wasn't the big three-0 or four-0. Everyone makes a big deal about them, but they don't bother me.

It's the birthdays that end in a nine that I've grown to dread. For the record, this particular one was my 39th.

I think turning thirty-nine is worse than turning forty because it's like someone's put up a great glaring neon sign highlighting the fact that the big one is only a year away. I went through the same thing on my 29th. During that birthday, and for most of the following year, I was hugely aware of the giant sword hanging over my head, with the imaginary voice of the executioner bellowing at me over and over:

"You're nearly thirty!"

"You're not young anymore!"

"It's all downhill from here!"

So depressing was the thought that at times I felt that he may as well chop my head off and be done with it. I remembered watching some old sci-fi movie when I was a kid when society did exactly that – kill everyone off at the age of thirty. On my gloomier days, it seemed like a perfectly sensible idea.

By the time thirty did roll around I'd had a whole year to come to terms with the situation so the day itself was not too bad after all. It was one of the few birthdays I had enjoyed since becoming an adult. Rob was exceptionally attentive by his standards – looking back, it was possibly the last year before he had started knocking off the neighbour because after that he didn't bother.

Once I had settled into my thirties I came to quite enjoy them. The whole decade stretched out in front of me, seemingly full of possibilities, which at that time included the very realistic prospect of marriage and babies. I came to realise that thirty was no age at all, not in the modern world.

Then the years flew by, and suddenly here I was hitting thirty-nine with another sword hanging over my head. This time the terrifying prospect of being forty was looming on the horizon. That was practically middle-aged. I thought back to when I was twenty-nine and how worried I had been about that. It all seemed quite laughable now. I hadn't been much more than a kid.

Now I was about to hit forty and what had I achieved in the past decade? Diddly-squat, that's what.

I had gone backwards if anything. I still had the same job, but not the same boyfriend, who I foolishly at one point believed might want to marry me and be the father of my babies. Now I didn't have a boyfriend at all.

My sex life was laughably non-existent, confined to my own solitary fumbling over countless unfulfilled fantasies and missed opportunities. As for my biological clock, that wasn't so much ticking as booming out like Big Ben's bongs as they heralded the dawn of yet another year.

Under the circumstances, there was no way I was making even a token effort to celebrate the dawn of the final year of my fourth decade. Some people were making a big deal out of it being the end of the first quarter of the century.

Where had all that time gone? It seemed like the Millennium had only just happened. It was all so depressing that when the holiday period roster was being drawn up at work, I was the first to put my name down.

Working four nights in a row was no sweat to me. I did it all the time. What did it matter? Without kids or a partner, it wasn't as if I was missing any quality time with anyone.

New Year wasn't the most pleasant time to be working in the hospital, but with the consolation of a week in Lanzarote just over a week away, I wasn't particularly bothered. It wasn't as if I was in A&E or anything – working there on New Year's Eve was, by all accounts, a nightmare.

Up on the wards, we just picked up the fallout. Some of those admitted through A&E found their way up to me. Many of them were the worse for wear due to drink – either imbibing too much of it or being assaulted by someone else who had. It was like this most weekends so I was used to it, but at New Year you could double it and then some.

The first such individual didn't even wait until New Year – a particularly unpleasant man who had nearly lost an eye in a pub brawl on the 30th. He was under the impression that swearing at the nurses was a good way to get what he wanted – as he swiftly found out, it was not.

He was typical of the drunks we got from time to time who seemed to think it was acceptable to get lippy with us. It was something I just wouldn't stand for. Having a go at people in the pub is bad enough, but abusing the trained healthcare professionals trying to patch them back together was way beyond out of order.

It wasn't unheard of for these dregs of humanity to even assault the staff, and following an incident the previous year, we'd had panic buttons installed on all the wards. Working for the NHS could be a thankless task at times, but as they say, somebody's gotta do it.

In my early years of nursing, I found these drunken, leery arseholes intimidating, but over the years I had learnt to give as good as I got. Anyone trying to backchat me soon got put in their place and there was very little they could say that would faze me. What did affect me was the other type of patient we saw more of at this time of year than any other.

I'm talking about the suicide cases – those poor, desperate souls who for whatever reason can't find the strength in themselves to face another year. It certainly puts my trivial New Year woes into perspective.

Thankfully, up on the wards I usually only get to see the survivors. If they make it as far as us, the vast majority do live to tell the tale. But I'm well aware that there are plenty more out there who won't be found in time.

This particular New Year's Eve featured examples of both types of cases. It was the third of my four nights and by dawn, we had four new patients on my ward – one with alcohol poisoning, another one who had been glassed in a fight in a pub, the second such case in as many nights, and another who had been beaten to a pulp in an argument over whose turn it was at a taxi rank.

The fourth was a single mother in her late-twenties who had taken an overdose of painkillers.

What had driven her to do that I didn't know at this stage but I hoped I would find out when she woke up. I took a tough line with the drunks and other idiots, but I could be equally tender with those who needed it. If I got the chance to talk with this girl the next day, I would do whatever I could to help her through her pain.

A tender hand was also needed for those who invariably came to us in the final days of their lives. We'd had one such patient on the ward for the past few days, a middle-aged man who was on the verge of succumbing, like so many before him, to the ravages of lung cancer.

I had grown to like Thomas Scott. Despite his terminal state of health, he had maintained his dignity and even a sense of humour, joking and even flirting with me a little as I cared for him. As the end neared I felt increasingly sorry for Thomas. He was only in his fifties which was far too young to die.

His daughter Stacey, a lovely and compassionate young woman, came in to see him every day. She was devoted to her father, and striking up a conversation with her I found out there had been a fair amount of tragedy in her life. Her mother had been killed by a drink-driver years before and now she was about to become an orphan in her twenties.

She, too, needed comfort, perhaps more so than Thomas who seemed to have accepted his fate. I was more than happy to be a shoulder to cry on, reflecting that it wasn't just the patients that needed help sometimes: it was also those closest to them.

Some of my colleagues held the opinion that we should keep a professional distance from our patients, including their nearest and dearest, but I didn't agree. This wasn't a production line in a factory – we were dealing with living, feeling human beings. Just by being in hospital they were in many cases going through some of the most traumatic moments of their lives, dying or otherwise.

I had come into caring after witnessing death and misery on a wide scale in my youth after a natural disaster. I realised then that what I wanted to do was care for those in need. If I was detached from people's emotional needs, then what was the point? I might as well go and stack shelves in Tesco.

I did a lot of caring that last, normal day. Just before I got off shift in the morning I spent some time with Kacey, the girl who had tried to take her own life during the Hogmanay celebrations. It came as no surprise to hear it was all over a man, who in this case had turned out to be a really nasty piece of work.

Over the course of about half an hour, she related the whole grisly tale to me. It seemed that she had been muddling along as a single mum until a couple of years ago when this lad, Aaron, had come into her life and swept her off her feet. But he hadn't been all he had appeared to be.

He had been a drug dealer and a criminal, who had gradually taken over her life, seducing her with money and glamour before hooking her on drugs so he could control her. He also used her flat to store his merchandise and when she eventually got raided following a tip-off, it was her, rather than him, that the police arrested.

With threats of violence, if she implicated him, Kacey ended up in court and fined, but it didn't end there. In a financial mess and drug-dependent, she had come to the attention of social services. Ultimately, her three-year-old daughter was taken away.

That had been the final nail in the coffin that had driven her to the overdose. Aaron, of course, was long gone by this time, having moved on to his next victim.

I tried to empathise with her situation as best as I could but my suffering at the hands of my unfaithful man was trivial compared to what she had been through. Remembering the heartbreak I had been through at New Year, four years ago, I could scarcely begin to imagine the extent of her pain.

I wanted to tell her it would get easier, but would it? She had pretty much lost everything. All I could do was counsel her and offer her advice on how to get clean and get her daughter back which had to be the number one priority.

After a few hours of sleep, I came back to work on the evening of 1st January for the last of my four nights. It turned out it was to be my last night in a way that I was completely unaware of yet. During this final shift, my world was going to be turned upside down.

On my return, I discovered that Thomas Scott was in a bad way. He was unconscious and near death. The strange events that were to change my life were destined to occur in his private room which was just off the main ward. It was paid for by the private healthcare he received as part of his pension package.

Apparently, he had had quite a stellar career in the retail trade and had retired early, clearly not short of a few quid. This was all information I had gleaned from one of my many chats with Stacey over the previous few days. Talking about her dad seemed to help her deal with what she was going through.

The last time I had spoken to Thomas himself had been on the morning of the 30th, just before I went off shift. He had been struggling that day, seemingly forgetful of who he was or why he was in hospital. Subsequently, he had gone quickly downhill. By the time I came into work that evening, it was clear he was not going to last the night.

The end came in the early hours of the following morning. I had been caring for him during the previous few hours but had gone for a break when the inevitable happened. It was left to my colleague Carmen to give me sad news when she returned to the break room.

"I'm afraid Mr Scott's just passed away," she said.

Some people think that we nurses become anaesthetised to such news, dealing with it every day. But I never did, and felt very sorry for Thomas and his family. He had been a decent guy.

"Did he regain consciousness at all?" I asked.

"He woke up briefly," replied Carmen. "He wasn't alone – his daughter was with him."

The task of preparing the body to be taken down to the mortuary fell to me. This was the one part of the job of nursing that I never felt fully prepared for, no matter how many times I did it.

On the way to Thomas's room, I passed Stacey and her fiancé, David. She looked up at me, her tear-stained face full of grief. She let go of David and hugged me.

"It's OK," I said as I held her, even though of course it wasn't.

Nothing could take away the pain of what she had just been through, but if I could offer even the slightest crumb of comfort just from the warmth of human contact then I had helped, albeit in a small way.

I approached Thomas's room, steeling myself for the sad task that lay ahead. The first thing I would do when I got into the room would be to open the window, even though it was freezing outside.

This was a nursing tradition that had been taught to me in my early days by an older nurse who I had worked with in Africa with the Red Cross. She was a committed Christian and had claimed that it would help to set the deceased's spirit free.

14

Although I wasn't much of a believer in the afterlife myself, it had stuck with me and it always felt like the right thing to do.

Next, I would begin the process of laying out the body. I would wash the patient from head to toe, and then dress him or her in fresh linen prior to the body being taken down to the morgue. As I went about this, I always treated the dead patient with the utmost respect, speaking gently to them as if they were still alive.

At odds with my generally atheist nature, at these moments there was always a small part of me that imagined some small spark of consciousness might still exist somewhere. If that were true, then hopefully my words of comfort might help them along on their journey to wherever they believed they might be going.

Or maybe I was just doing it to help me cope better with the task at hand. Either way, it worked for me.

I was not destined to even get started on these tasks this time. As I opened the door to the private room I was taken aback to see a very oddly dressed stranger inside, peering intently at the chart of the bottom of Thomas's bed.

He was dressed in outdoor clothing but with an old-fashioned medical white coat draped over the top. If this was some attempt to disguise himself as a doctor it was a pretty lame one, particularly as he was also wearing a large hiker's rucksack over the top of the coat.

My first thought on seeing the rucksack was of terrorism. It was a reaction I always had now when I saw anyone acting even slightly out of the ordinary wearing a rucksack. It was an irrational fear brought on by decades of terrorist attacks in London and elsewhere.

This man didn't look like your average terrorist, whatever that was. I suppose my fears had conditioned me to imagine some young man of Middle Eastern origin. This was prejudiced, I know, but too many images in the media had imprinted this cliché indelibly in my mind.

This man was white and middle-aged – in his early fifties at a guess. Not only did he not look like a terrorist, but also it was illogical to even think that he might be. Why would anyone want to blow up an empty hospital room with nothing but a dead body and a cheap, plastic Christmas tree in it?

Whoever he was, he ought not to be there, and I had no hesitation in challenging him.

"Who are you?" I demanded, determined not to show any fear despite the distinctly uneasy feeling flooding through my body. "What are you doing in here?"

"I'm Doctor Gardner," he said, in a ludicrously posh accent that just had to be put on as he cast his gaze down at my name badge. "I'm a specialist, visiting from Harley Street. I'm delighted to meet you, Amy."

I wasn't convinced for a moment by his overblown acting. Who did he think he was, Hugh Grant? I was also not impressed by him ogling my breasts during his laughably poor performance.

"Don't give me that," I replied, "and stop staring at my tits. None of the doctors in this hospital or anywhere else wear white coats anymore. What they do wear is ID, so where's yours?"

"Ah yes, one of the chaps down on security was going to print it off for me earlier this evening," he ventured. "I must pop down and pick it up at some point."

I just looked at him with a face that said, "Really?" I didn't even have to utter the word. He could see I didn't believe a word of it and changed tack.

"Look, I'll come clean," he said, reverting to a normal accent. "I'm not a doctor, I'm a scientist attached to the university carrying out some research here. I just need a couple of minutes, that's all. Then I'll be out of your hair."

Was he telling the truth? With his backpack along with waving a strange metal, wand-like device around in front of him, I guess he could pass for a scientist, but not a lucid and bona fide one. He looked more like some crazy character from a sci-fi movie. All he was lacking was the wild, Einstein-style hair.

A more likely explanation was that he was some sort of escaped mental patient and if that was the case, I could well be in danger. Mindful of last year's incident on the ward, I decided the best course of action would be to call for some help.

"I'm sorry, that's not good enough," I replied. "People don't go around hospitals in the middle of the night wearing dubious disguises unless they're up to no good."

"What can I get up to in here?" protested the fake Doctor Gardner, gesturing towards the body on the bed. "It's not as if I've come to bump him off, is it? It's a bit late for that: the Grim Reaper's already been and gone."

"I'm calling security," I replied, moving towards the telephone on the wall beside the door.

"No, don't do that," he protested and began to move to cut me off. That was all the provocation I needed. Issuing a silent prayer of thanks for the recently improved security measures, I headed for the panic button on the wall behind the bed instead, reaching it just before he was able to stop me.

His attempt to block my path had been more than a little unsettling. I hoped that whoever was on security was paying attention and not snoozing on the job.

Doctor Gardner, if that was his real name, backed off once he saw the flashing red button on the wall.

"Since when have hospitals had panic buttons?" he asked, looking unsettled.

He was on the back foot all of a sudden which gave me a chance to seize the initiative. I had no intention of showing him any weakness so, keeping my voice as level as I could, I spelled out the situation in black and white.

"Since last year when a patient assaulted a nurse on this very ward," I replied. "Do you have any idea how much abuse we get from the drunks that get hauled in here every weekend? Now you've got less than two minutes until security arrives from downstairs to escort you from the premises – and that won't be pleasant. They don't take too kindly to women being threatened and can get quite heavy-handed. If I were you, I would scarper now, while you still can."

This was a blatant lie. The ageing head of security, Barry, spent the vast majority of his time sitting in his office drinking tea and eating biscuits. He hadn't seen any action since his Army days, decades in the past. Most of his colleagues were no better. But this stranger wasn't to know that.

"Fine," he said, "but I'll be back and you won't even know about it."

I assumed that meant he was going to leave, but he didn't show any signs of departing by the traditional method, i.e. through the door. Instead, he pointed his weird device in front of him and started pressing buttons on it. It was the first time I had seen it and it looked like something out of *Doctor Who*.

"What are you doing?" I asked, becoming increasingly convinced that he was some sort of nutter.

"Nothing for you to worry about," was his reply.

This man had seriously lost the plot. What did he think he was going to do – teleport out of there with his home-made remote control TV aerial?

Ironically, outlandish as that idea had seemed at the time, given what happened next I may not have been far off the mark. Because this was the moment when the weird sci-fi shit started happening, leading me to realise that he was more than just a weirdo after all. Of course, it was too late to do anything about it by then. I was caught up in whatever was going on and it was too late to avoid it. I was well and truly over my event horizon.

What happened was all over very quickly. Suddenly there seemed to be two of him in the room, the second one seemingly appearing out of nowhere. He hadn't come through the door, that's for sure, as I would have seen him from where I was standing.

This other version looked identical, right down to the white coat. Could they be twins or was it some kind of visual trickery? There was no time to figure it out as something else was already happening.

They had both been pointing their wands across the room, close to Thomas's bed. Then I heard a long-drawn-out cry of "Nooooo!" from one or possibly both of the men, in the style of some overly dramatic movie scene. I might have found this amusing if I had been watching from afar, rather than being an unwilling participant.

Then everything descended into a kaleidoscopic, whirling maelstrom of colour and noise. As multiple mirror images of myself, the stranger and the body on the bed swirled all around me, I felt myself being sucked by a hugely powerful force towards the centre of the room.

Like a spider in a bathtub being drawn towards the plughole, I flailed my arms helplessly, completely powerless to escape. It was the last thing I remembered before I blacked out.

And that is how all of this began.

Chapter Three
2023

When I woke up the first time after it happened I was disorientated, panicky and confused. It was similar to that feeling you get when waking up from a very vivid dream or nightmare.

Just as with one of those dreams, for the first few seconds of consciousness, everything that had happened seemed real. Then, as familiar surroundings reasserted themselves, reality began to kick back in.

The sense of relief that it had all been just a dream washed over me. That feeling was to be only temporary. The events of the next hour or so would see to that.

The reassuringly safe place I found myself in was my bedroom in my flat in Headington, an area to the north of Oxford. It was purpose-built accommodation for nurses, less than half a mile from the John Radcliffe Hospital.

I shared the flat with two other girls and it had been my home for nearly four years, since shortly after my pig of an ex had done the dirty on me. This had left me needing to find somewhere else to live in a hurry.

The ultimate result was that I found myself going the wrong way on the property ladder, from being a homeowner back to renting. This was not something you wanted to be doing in a place like Oxford where house prices marched relentlessly upwards, regardless of the state of the economy.

Fortunately for me, at least in the short term, I was not to end up homeless. A new government, determined to tackle the inequality in society created by the runaway housing market, had decided to take decisive action. In addition to building a million new council homes over four years, they had pledged millions of pounds towards an enhanced key worker scheme.

This was designed to help nurses, teachers and other professionals to have somewhere to live in areas where they were priced out of the housing market. Oxford was just about the most unaffordable place in the country to live based on the ratio of housing costs to average wages and had been one of the first to be chosen for the scheme.

This meant a new programme of building social housing specifically for people like me. It had created a home for me, Phoebe and Lily, three single nurses, for which we paid the very reasonable sum of £325 a month each in rent.

The downside was that the flat came with the job – so I was stuck with nursing for life now unless I won the lottery. That didn't bother me for now as I enjoyed my job, but I didn't like the prospect of being tied to it permanently. What if I wanted a change of career later on?

The flat we lived in was one of several in a new ultra-high-tech building. It had been built on the site of an old tower block which had been condemned and demolished over fire safety concerns after a catastrophic fire in a similar London structure a few years previously.

Our state-of-the-art new home was just about as eco-friendly as you could get. From solar panels on the roof to a rain-harvesting system, every resource was maximised. The government had dubbed them the homes of the future and dozens of them were now going up in cities all over Britain.

Phoebe and Lily were younger than me, in their mid-twenties, but the age gap hadn't been a problem. I had taken on a new lease of life since I had split with Rob and it was as if those nine years wasted on him had never happened.

Far from finding my energetic, young flatmates annoying, I found their various antics amusing and, despite all being strangers when we moved in, we soon became firm friends. They were outsiders in Oxford, just as I had once been, and we gelled almost straight away.

There was certainly a lively mix of accents in the house. Although I had lived in Oxford for many years, my Scouse accent still prevailed, and along with Lily – a Geordie, and Phoebe, from Cornwall, we had at least three corners of England covered.

Being younger they hadn't got themselves tied up in any emotional baggage yet, so were still carefree, fit and up for fun.

Lily was the elder of the two, a small pixie-like girl with elfish features and black hair that curled down in small tangles around her face. She loved to wear old-fashioned, hippyish clothes, with flowers in her hair and plenty of necklaces and bracelets. She was also adorned all over with tattoos, which I had to admit were tastefully done, even though tattoos had never been my thing.

Despite being only twenty-seven she had a taste for the older, indie music that her parents had brought her up on. The tunes of The Cure, New Order and The Mission could often be heard blaring out from her room.

"I'm a girl out of time," she once said to me. "My mother saw all of these bands at Glastonbury in the late-80s. If I had a time machine and could go back in time, that's where I'd go. People knew how to enjoy themselves in those days."

Lily loved her festivals and had tried to persuade me many times to go to Glastonbury or Reading with her. I had resisted, being a little too fond of my creature comforts and adequate toilet facilities to want to rough it there. She assured me that it wasn't like that anymore and I could have all mod cons if I wanted them. I had never been to a festival, so in the end, I agreed and all three of us had begun making plans to go the following year.

Phoebe, at twenty-five, was a couple of years younger than Lily and had been newly qualified as a nurse when we had moved into the flat. Her look was a complete contrast to Lily's. She was blonde and carrying a few extra pounds, but in a way that complemented her figure, rather than making her look overweight. She had a youthful chubbiness that gave her curves in all the right places and boobs to die for, as well as a rounded, welcoming face.

She had a much more relaxed attitude to clothing in comparison to Lily's elaborate outfits. For Phoebe, it was T-shirts and joggers most of the time when she was just slobbing around the flat. She rarely wore a bra at home and it wasn't unknown for her to wander around the flat half-naked in the summertime. I wasn't bothered about that at all, but it irked Lily who was relatively flat-chested by comparison.

Although I didn't have any leanings towards women, I couldn't help admiring Phoebe's confidence in her body, and those tits – well, they were pretty awesome and I didn't mind seeing them on display. I had a decent pair myself, so I had been told, but Phoebe's put mine to shame. They seemed to defy gravity, unlike mine which were starting to sag with age.

Phoebe's exhibitionism didn't do any harm as far as I was concerned. We were all confirmed heterosexuals and all single – which made for a lot of fun. We would go out together on the nights when we were all off work and it wasn't unusual for one of us to bring someone back.

More often than not it was Phoebe, which meant that Lily and I would need to put our earphones in for the night. Phoebe's uninhibited nature also meant she didn't hold back on the noise when she was enjoying the attentions of a man.

It was rare for me to pull these days, but I didn't mind as the three of us were having a lot of fun. It was without doubt the best time I'd had for years but it came with a price. At the back of my mind, was the endless tick-tock, tick-tock of the biological clock. It went hand in hand with a feeling that perhaps I ought not to be doing this sort of thing at my age.

It was alright for Lily and Phoebe – they had time on their side – but I was a late thirty-something playing at being their age and I knew I couldn't keep it up forever.

The age gap didn't manifest itself in our day-to-day interactions but there was one activity that really showed it up. When we went clubbing, the girls seemed to be able to dance away all night, just as I had at their age. But that was fifteen years ago and now my body was protesting in no uncertain terms. My feet were aching after about half an hour, the music was dreadful and too loud, and there was never anywhere to sit down.

Often on these nights out I secretly wished I was at home having a cup of tea and watching *Coronation Street* on catch-up. I tried to brush these thoughts off, reminding myself that I was enjoying the last gasp of what little youth I had left and I should be making the most of it because soon it would be gone.

I hadn't known then that I was wrong about that – how could I? I knew nothing about the life-changing event which was soon to restore my youth to me. But I was about to find out because it was on this particular morning that my peculiar new back-to-front existence began.

I didn't realise right away that anything was wrong – I was where I woke up every day, after all, but then I realised that I couldn't remember anything about going to bed the previous day. I remembered all that weird stuff from the hospital room but still thought that had been a dream at this point, despite its continuing presence in my mind. I cast my mind back, trying to figure it all out.

I recalled being at work but nothing afterwards – certainly nothing about finishing work and going home. I felt rough and incredibly groggy as I sat up in the room, trying to get my head together. Was this a hangover?

There had been more than one occasion I had woken up in my life so hung-over that I couldn't recall the details of what had gone on the night before. Unfortunately, cameras often caught the sordid evidence for all to see and there were frequent occasions when I would open up my social media dreading what I was going to find.

Often it didn't make for pleasant viewing – some bleary-eyed photos of myself with random people, half of whom I didn't even know, or some drunken, ridiculous comments on a Facebook status that I recall neither reading nor writing.

Was today one such occasion? It was hard to see how it could be. I had been working nights, and unlike some of my colleagues who considered a pint in Wetherspoons to be an acceptable end to a night's work, I preferred to go straight home and go to bed.

The only other possibility was that I'd had a total blackout and somehow lost an entire day but I'd never been that drunk before, even in the wildest days of my youth. If that was the reason why I was in this state, then my flatmates were bound to have been involved. They liked to party and it wasn't inconceivable that they had got me so paralytic on my birthday that I couldn't remember what I'd done.

There was only one thing to do – I would have to go out there and face the two of them. If I had done something embarrassingly awful, they would know about it. But to prepare myself, I would first check social media for clues about any possible indiscretions. That meant I needed my phone. I had been lying on my back for about five minutes pondering all this, but now I sat up, ready to face the music.

The curtains were drawn but they were pale lemon in colour which let through a small amount of daylight. It was just enough light for me to locate my phone on the bedside table, plugged into its charger. Like a lot of people, I ignored the advice not to have electronic gadgets in the bedroom, unable to bear being more than a few feet away from my phone at any one time.

I managed to get hold of it, but couldn't get past the screen lock. It usually operated on a thumbprint, but that wasn't working for some reason. It was asking for a PIN. I tried the one I had used on my old phone, 0101, and it let me in.

Yes, I know 0101 is my birthday and I shouldn't use it because it's the first thing hackers try, but I've tried using other numbers and I just end up forgetting them. It's the same reason I use the same password for all my internet stuff which is the name of my first cat plus the year of my birth. I'd never keep track of it all otherwise.

Using the name of one's pet isn't necessarily a good idea either, but I gave that cat a pretty unusual name which I doubt many would be able to guess. So I don't have to worry about anyone guessing it. It's been good enough up until now because I've not been defrauded of anything, at least not that I know of.

Having managed to get past my own security, I realised quite quickly that it wasn't just the missing thumbprint scan that was up with my phone. The background picture was also wrong. I'd changed it to a picture of me and the girls on a night out before Christmas a couple of weeks ago. Now it had changed back to a picture of my old cat, Tommy.

I know what you're thinking – that's not an unusual name for a cat, but before anyone starts trying to empty my bank account, I should point out I am not talking about the same cat. Tommy was my most recent pet whom I miss terribly.

I had to have him rehomed because the new flats don't allow pets and my selfish ex-fiancé didn't want him. The only pussy he was interested in was the one belonging to Emma next door. That's a lame pun, I know, and it makes me sound bitter, but somehow making light of it crudely like this seems to help.

I hadn't used this picture of Tommy for ages, not since I'd changed phones. It had been the wallpaper on my old phone. Come to think of it, now I looked more closely, this was my old phone.

This was a Samsung S12, not an S13. Why did I have this old phone? I'd upgraded a couple of months ago and kept this one as a backup. As soon as my new one was up and running, the S12 had been chucked unceremoniously into the same drawer where I put all my old phones, destined never to see the light of day again. I had quite a collection, going way back to my first Nokia. I had meant to chuck them all out when I moved here, but for whatever reason could not part with them.

But now here it was, the S12, in my hand. Had I lost my new one while I was out doing whatever I had been doing and started using this one again? And if so, why couldn't I remember anything about it? Was this down to my suspected blackout or was it something more?

My memories were scrambled and I couldn't retrieve them. It was like sitting in front of a laptop waiting for it to respond while that bloody annoying hourglass thing spins hopelessly round and round in circles.

This wouldn't do at all. My memories refused to come. I still felt groggy and half-asleep which wasn't helping matters. What had I done yesterday to make me feel like this?

I got up and felt my way across the floor in the semi-darkness, taking care not to trip over any discarded clothes or shoes on the floordrobe. Reaching the window I pulled aside the curtains to let the weak winter sunlight flood into the room.

If I had hoped that this might shed some light on my situation, I was mistaken. The same question kept repeating over and over in my head.

What the hell was I doing last night?

I tried again to piece it together, but my memory was still eluding me. I was sure I had been at work, so how did I end up getting drunk? Could I really have gone on a bender afterwards? I had never done that while working nights and I had been doing them for many years.

Vivid memories from the dream that had seemed so lifelike earlier began to spill into my head again – multiple images of a man holding a futuristic TV aerial and a dead body on a bed, all spinning round in circles but now they were laughing at me, mocking me as I was sucked into – well, whatever it was I had been sucked into.

It was just a dream – wasn't it? If so, it had been unlike any other one I had ever had and it was also disturbing that it was not fading away into my subconscious after a few minutes awake. If anything, my recollections were getting stronger.

I sat back down on the bed which took up a good two-thirds of the floor space in the room. The new flats may have been super eco-friendly but the bedrooms were also what an estate agent might generously describe as bijou. Space was at a premium and it didn't help that I'd opted to buy a king-size bed for my room.

In hindsight, that had been pretty optimistic. I hadn't been a complete nun since I'd split up with Rob, but Phoebe and

Lily got a lot more use out of their double beds than I got out of my king-size.

Between the end of the bed and the wardrobe was barely three feet of floor space. As I sat on the end of the bed, I looked up at my close-up reflection on the wardrobe door mirror. Now there was something else that caught my eye.

As on most nights when I was on my own, I had slept in just knickers and an old T-shirt. But this one was exceptionally old. In fact, it was so old that I was pretty sure I had thrown it out about six months ago.

It was an ancient *Angry Birds* T-shirt that I'd bought more than a decade ago when the game had been huge. By the time I reluctantly parted with it, it was pretty much falling apart. The only good thing I could say about it during its final days was that the holes under the armpits were very handy for applying deodorant.

I thought again. Had I really thrown it out? I was sure I had. It certainly wasn't in any fit state to be reused so I wouldn't have taken it to a charity shop. They would undoubtedly have refused it, which would have been plain embarrassing. So how come I was wearing it now?

First the mystery over the phone and now this. I needed answers so I headed for the bedroom door and out into the main part of the flat. As I opened the door I was greeted by the unmistakeably gorgeous smell of freshly cooked bacon.

I loved the design of our flat. It was neatly split in two, with all the bedrooms plus the bathroom on one side, and the living space on the other. When you walked in through the front door, the left-hand side was almost like walking down a corridor in a hotel, with four doors, one after another. In order, these went bathroom, Lily's room, Phoebe's room, and my room.

Lily felt she had the best room, as it was nearest the bathroom, but I liked mine because being on the end it had the bigger window and a better view. I could see the park from my room, but all they could see were the flats opposite.

The right-hand side of the flat was all open-plan, with just a small breakfast bar as a divider between the kitchen and the rest of the living space. The kitchen was closest to the front of the flat, opposite the bathroom and Lily's room, followed by a small dining area, and then the living area which in estate agent terminology was positively spacious compared to the bedrooms.

That living room was the hub of our little home, and it was there that I now found Phoebe and Lily camped out in front of the television, sitting with the curtains closed watching some old Disney film, a staple of the Christmas and New Year TV schedules. A familiar battered, old, fake Christmas tree stood next to the TV, fairy lights twinkling on and off in a preordained sequence. It was refreshingly normal after my dream and the other odd things I had noticed this morning.

"Oh, look, it stirs," said Lily, catching sight of me as I padded, barefoot, into the living space. "You look a bit rough, pet."

We had an orange, L-shaped sofa in one corner of the room and Lily was slumped at one end of it, blanket over her, sipping a mug of coffee. I had never known anyone drink as much coffee as Lily. She seemed to live on the stuff and I had rarely seen her eat. I had also never heard her address anyone by their real name. Phoebe and I were both addressed as "pet" as was the postman and pretty much anyone else we ever came into contact with.

At the other end of the sofa, leaning over the coffee table, wolfing down a toasted bacon sandwich, was Phoebe. It wasn't difficult to see how she maintained her full figure.

"Is there any of that left?" I asked, knowing what the answer would be before the words were even out of my mouth.

"Sorry," said Phoebe, in her strong, West Country dialect. "There were only five rashers left and I always have at least three so I thought I may as well finish it off. No point leaving two, is there?"

"I'd have been happy with two," I said. "Most people would."

"I can go to the shops and get you some more if you like?" she suggested, looking a little crestfallen. To her credit, Phoebe was good like that. She might eat all the food in the flat, including your own, but she always replaced it.

"No, you're OK," I said. "I'll just have some toast."

"Ah…" began Phoebe. "I kind of…"

"…finished the bread, too?" I suggested.

"Yeah, I'm really sorry, Amy. Look. I'm planning on going out and doing a big shop today. It's New Year tomorrow so most of the shops will be closed and we want to make sure we've got plenty in for your birthday."

"That's right," piped up Lily, turning to face me properly for the first time. "We're feeling really bad about forgetting last year and we want to make this one special for you."

After I had come into the room, which had initially seemed to be a picture of normality, my earlier confusion had temporarily abated. Now in the space of a few seconds, I had been hit with a double whammy that set off alarm bells in my head that screamed out *Something's wrong here*.

The first cue to unsettle me was what they had just said, but that was overshadowed by Lily's appearance. When I first came into the room I had only briefly clocked her, sitting in the semi-darkness, but now she was facing me I noticed her hair. Her hair was all wrong.

32

Leaving that aside for a moment, what they had both just said about my birthday had completely thrown me.

"Whoa, hold on a minute," I replied. "What are you talking about? My birthday was yesterday."

"Ha ha – that's a good one, Amy," said Phoebe. "Is this your way of trying to get out of it? You said your birthday was always rubbish, so we've decided that this year we are going to change that."

"But my birthday is 1st January," I protested. "It's 2nd January today."

"Umm, I don't think it is," replied Phoebe. "Didn't you hear what I said before? I told you I was going shopping for New Year food and drink today. Honestly, Amy, you never seem to listen to a word I say."

"Look, what's going on here?" I asked, perplexed. "Is this some sort of wind-up?"

If my head had been whirling gently before like that hourglass on a laptop, it had now accelerated to the proportions of an F5 tornado. Could this really be some sort of elaborate wind-up, or was I going to have to face the possibility that something seriously weird had happened to me?

Would they really have gone to the lengths of swapping my phone, digging my old T-shirt out of the bin, and then pretending the date was different? And what would be the point anyway? We weren't averse to playing pranks on each other. These ranged from the small ones, such as substituting Lily's beloved coffee with a decaffeinated blend to see if she noticed (she did), to the more elaborate ones.

For example, there was the stunt Lily and I pulled on Phoebe on Bonfire Night a couple of years ago. We spent all day creating our very own stuffed guy, complete with a strap-on dildo and put it on Phoebe's bed, ready for when she got home from work.

She called our bluff on that occasion and when we dared her to ride it, she went and did it. Not with us in the room, obviously – that would have been seriously weird, but she still did it. That was Phoebe all over – always up for anything.

"OK, guys, you got me," I said. "What's this supposed to be – some sort of weird time travel thing?"

Then I remembered what it was that had struck me about Lily's appearance a few moments before.

"You didn't have to go to that extent of putting the dreadlocks back in your hair, though, Lily. That must have taken hours."

She had worn dreads the past year or two but had decided to dispense with them last summer.

"What are you on about, pet?" said Lily. "I've had these for a couple of years. Though I am thinking of getting rid of them – I fancy a new look. What do you think?"

Neither of them looked like they were playing a prank, especially Phoebe who could never keep a straight face for long when mischief was afoot.

My eyes were drawn to the TV in the corner, where the film had finished and the BBC News had come on. A reporter was standing outside Big Ben talking about preparations for the New Year fireworks.

For the first time, I began to suspect this wasn't a wind-up. It couldn't be. Surely they wouldn't have gone to the effort of recording that and then playing it back just to confuse me. It went way beyond anything we had done before. It seemed that I had to contemplate the possibility that unless something had seriously gone wrong with my mind somehow I had travelled back two days in time.

But that didn't explain Lily's hair – it was months since she had disposed of the dreads.

Then I caught sight of the calendar on the wall, and there it was, staring at me in a big, black, bold font: confirmation that I really had gone back in time.

The month showing on the calendar was December 2023 which was consistent with Lily's appearance.

I hadn't gone back two days in time.

I had gone back more than a year.

Chapter Four
2023

"I need to go back to my room," I said, flustered. "I'm feeling a bit sick."

I wasn't lying. The enormity of what might be happening was making me feel quite nauseous. I needed some time to try to make sense of it all.

"Do you want me to get you anything from the pharmacy when I go to Sainsbury's?" asked Phoebe.

Good old Phoebe. Despite being the youngest, she often mothered me and Lily.

"No, don't worry. I'll be alright later. I just need a bit of a lie-down," I said. "I didn't sleep very well last night."

"Well, make sure you're fighting fit for tonight," said Lily. "Double celebrations, remember?"

"I'm so glad we're not working this year," added Phoebe. "Not after Tessa getting assaulted on the ward on Christmas Eve. It's not safe at this time of year."

I might not remember much about my own last few hours, but if this was a year ago, then what they were saying made sense. This year had been that rarest of things, a New Year that I had genuinely enjoyed. The girls had persuaded me not to sign up for work and to go out with them instead.

It had been pretty decent, all things considered. They had even remembered to wish me Happy Birthday at midnight despite their intoxication, a rarity indeed.

As for Tessa, she had been the nurse attacked on the wards by a drunken punter, the very incident that had led to the panic buttons being put in. Phoebe mentioning this was just one more piece of evidence that I had travelled back to 2023.

"I'm looking forward to it," I said, recalling a few vague details of that night out, which for me was a year ago. I was probably looking forward to it more than I had been the first time around when I had approached it with apprehension. This time, I had no such qualms. I knew it would turn out fine because it already had.

How strange was this going to be, living the same night out over again? Perhaps I could even improve on it now I had a second bite at the cherry. That's if I could remember all of it. It's surprising how much you forget in a year, and it didn't help that this had been one of those occasions when alcohol had also blurred the details.

I made my way back into my room, lay down on the bed and tried to get my dizzy, confused head in order.

Everything I had seen pointed to me being transported back in time by just over a year. The calendar and the conversation made me pretty certain it was 31st December 2023. I reached over for my phone for confirmation.

Yep, there it was, crystal-clear on the 4k display. It seemed beyond doubt now that I had gone back in time.

I had no idea of the actual mechanics that had caused this unlikely event but I wasn't unfamiliar with the whole concept of time travel. From *The Time Traveler's Wife* to *About Time*, I had seen and enjoyed all the movies. I had always thought of them as pure fantasy and never in my wildest imagination had I ever believed I might find myself in such a situation myself. But here I was.

My presence here in the past was almost certainly something to do with the mysterious "Doctor Gardner", as he had called himself. Whatever he had done in that room back at the hospital hadn't been a dream at all – it really had happened and it had brought me back here.

So what had happened to him? Had he been transported back in time, too? And if so, where was he? Not here, that was for sure. Might he be at the hospital still? Was it worth going to look?

What about me? Where was my younger self? If my body had been transported back here, shouldn't there also have been a younger version of myself sleeping in this very bed when I woke up? The questions were being fired at me faster than Bradley Walsh on *The Chase*, and I couldn't answer any of them.

Clearly, there wasn't another me here so maybe there was another explanation. I sat up and looked closely at myself in the mirror. Had all of me been transported back, or was it just my mind? Did my soul now inhabit the body of my younger self?

It was impossible to tell just by looking in the mirror. I looked the same as I expected to, but then people don't age that much in a year. Unlike Lily, I didn't radically alter my hair, get new tattoos, or make any other radical changes in my appearance on a regular basis, so there were no clues there. I didn't feel any different either.

Funny, isn't it, how as people we barely change from one year to the next, yet over time small changes imperceptibly mount up? Put two photographs of any adult taken a year apart next to each other and you'd struggle to pick which one was older. Try the same thing with two pictures separated by a decade and it would be quite a different story.

What little evidence I had to go on led me to conclude that I was in my younger body. I based that primarily on the lack of a counterpart and that I was wearing my old T-shirt. This wasn't necessarily a bad thing.

The more I thought about it, the more I concluded that there wasn't anything bad about this at all. Yes, it was unsettling and disorientating, but it seemed I had been given a whole year of my life to live over again and who wouldn't take that if it were offered? The richest person in the world couldn't buy that.

Whether it had been a good or a bad year wouldn't matter. If it had been a bad one, then surely it could all be turned around with the foreknowledge of what was to come. And a good year – well, that could always be made even better.

From my perspective, it hadn't been either of those things. If I had to sum it up, 2024 had been a nondescript year. I hadn't really done or achieved anything. It had been mediocre to average, pretty much like every other year.

Sleep, work, eat, and repeat would pretty much sum up the year 2024. I had to be brutally honest with myself and admit that this was no good at all. I was drifting inexorably towards my forties just existing.

Sure, I'd had a laugh with Phoebe and Lily, lots of fun nights out and occasional brief dalliances with the opposite sex, but nothing that could be called progress. Perhaps with a year to live over again, I could rectify that.

One of my dalliances had been with Ben, a young doctor on the ward who had been pretty keen on me. He was only thirty-one and Phoebe and Lily had teased me, referring to him as my toy boy.

I think they were jealous and wouldn't have minded a piece of him themselves, but unusually, it was me he asked for a date. Flattered at being chosen over my younger, more nubile flatmates, I accepted.

On our first date, he told me he had a thing about the Scouse accent. For once, it had done me a favour. Most of the time when I was growing up, the well-spoken Oxfordshire kids had taken the piss out of it.

I was pretty keen on Ben, too, but had tried to play it cool, treating it as just a bit of fun, wary of getting serious with anyone again after what had happened with Rob. It was to prove my undoing as I played hard to get rather too long and paid the price.

When he got offered a post in London, he felt there was nothing to keep him in Oxford and he accepted, disappearing from my life before I'd had a chance to get to know him properly.

It had all been my fault, too – turning him down for dates, refuting romantic gestures and pretending I wasn't interested in anything other than the odd casual night in the sack – something at which Ben had been very proficient, I ought to add – far better than Rob.

What had I been thinking of? It's no wonder I had been single for four years. I would never have spurned an opportunity like this in the past but what had happened with Rob had tainted my judgement. The bastard was still messing up my head and my life even now, over three years since I had had any contact with him.

Ben and I had stayed in touch on Facebook but judging by the selfies he was posting of him and his new flame down in London, that ship had well and truly sailed.

Perhaps now I had this second chance I could change all that. If I had this year to live over again, could I not play my cards differently and not let him slip through my fingers this time?

What else could I change? If only I had known I was coming back here, I could have written down the EuroMillions numbers and then life could have been one big party. I was never going to get rich working shifts at the hospital and my lack of financial security wasn't painting a very rosy picture for my old age.

I was already worried I was going to end up as one of those old grannies hunched over an ancient, three-bar fire, having to make the grim choice between keeping warm or eating.

Technically, I wouldn't even be a granny due to my lack of kids. Who would be there for me in my old age? I was already an orphan, and my sister had been missing, presumed dead, since 2004. I was in danger of facing a lonely old age and it was a depressing thought.

Could I make any money any other way out of my little trek back through time? I thought about investing or betting, but since I took little interest in sport and none whatsoever in financial markets, I didn't know where to start. I struggled, trying to recall anything notable that had happened over the year that might offer me a chance to make some money.

I knew the Olympics had been on in Paris and the England football team had been in some big tournament or other. They had done badly because Barry on security at work had been ranting and raving about it. Who was it they had lost to? The Faroe Islands, wasn't it?

I didn't even know where the Faroe Islands were and was equally clueless when it came to understanding how betting worked, but I remember people saying it was the biggest shock ever in the history of football. That meant I would get good odds on it, wouldn't I?

I'd have plenty of time to figure it out because from what I remembered, the football had been in the summer. For now, all of this deep thinking about my situation had tired me out, so I lay back down and fell asleep.

I was out for quite some time because by the time I woke up again, it was dusk and I felt ravenously hungry. I ventured back out into the flat to see what the others were doing.

There was no sign of Lily, but I could hear a telltale buzzing coming from Phoebe's room so I knew not to disturb her. I wandered into the kitchen and opened the fridge to find it packed solid with food – meats, cheeses, pork pies and pretty much everything you would need to make a top-notch buffet. Phoebe had been true to her word.

She had also restocked the bread so I made myself a sandwich and sat down in front of the TV for a while, idly flicking through the channels. After my extended sleep, I was feeling quite relaxed about everything. In fact, I was pretty excited.

I had been given the gift of a whole year to live again which opened up all sorts of possibilities. I was going to go out tonight and really celebrate my birthday, much more than I had the first time round. Then I had only really been going through the motions for Phoebe and Lily's benefit, even if I had begrudgingly started to enjoy it as the alcohol began to flow. But now I had something to look forward to.

That's what I thought, anyway. But perhaps I shouldn't have made so many assumptions about my situation. Little did I know, in another couple of days, my fledgling plans for the year would be well and truly blown out of the water.

For the moment I was blissfully unaware of all that and consequently entered into my New Year's night out in a spirit I hadn't felt for years. I decided not to use my future knowledge to try and change anything about the evening but to just let things happen exactly as they did before – it was a sort of experiment, I suppose, to see if everything was identical or whether my foreknowledge would lead to inevitable changes.

As far as I can recall, we went to the same places as before – a restaurant and a bar down Little Clarendon Street. I couldn't remember the minutiae of what had happened a year ago, so it was going to be difficult to judge whether or not the evening would be a carbon copy of before.

The excessive alcohol consumption on both occasions didn't help matters. This time, I probably drank more than the first time around, as in my unusually euphoric state I kicked things off by ordering a bottle of champagne as soon as we got in the restaurant.

I realised at that early stage that things would not be precisely the same as before, because I hadn't ordered the champagne before. I simply wasn't in as big a party mood as I was this time. But would that invariably mean that the whole evening would deviate from that point onwards or not? Perhaps minor details like this wouldn't affect the ultimate course of the evening.

Our conversation was probably different, too, but I can't honestly remember what we talked about the first time around. Who does recall details of conversations a year later? It was highly unlikely I would have said word for word what I had the year before owing to my changed mindset.

Still, what did it matter? All I was concerned with was having a good time, so after a while, I stopped overanalysing and just concentrated on enjoying myself.

I was pleased and flattered when on the stroke of midnight, Phoebe and Lily screamed out "Happy Birthday!" at me, and simultaneously planted big, sloppy kisses on opposite cheeks. I remembered then that they had done the same thing the year before.

So I might have said my lines differently all evening from those in my previous performance, but the end result was the same. So it seems the small ripples in time I had created had not had any long-term effect on the timeline.

The next day was just as fun. We chilled out in our PJs in the flat and Phoebe laid out all the food she had bought on the breakfast bar before bringing in her pièce de résistance – a cake she had baked herself in the shape of a rippling, naked Adonis with bumps in all the right places. It was so good that even Lily asked for a second slice and she hardly ever ate anything.

Later, some other nurse friends who lived in the same building called around and we proceeded to get sloshed all over again.

I went to bed happier that birthday night than I had been in years. I was completely accepting of my new and strange situation and bursting with ideas and plans for the year ahead. I had been itching to tell the others what had happened to me so that they could share in my adventure, but I managed to resist the temptation. At best, they would have just thought it was another prank, at worst that I'd completely lost my marbles.

Yes, they'd probably seen and enjoyed all the same time-travel movies I had but they were just stories. No one was going to take seriously anyone who claimed something like that was actually happening to them in real life. I wouldn't have done either, before all of this.

No, I would keep it all to myself for the moment. If I felt the need to confide in one or both of my flatmates later, I'd have to try and come up with some sort of irrefutable proof, but I was tired and drunk right now and there would be plenty of time for all that later.

Or so I thought. What I didn't know when I fell asleep that night was that my world was about to be turned upside down all over again.

I knew something was wrong as soon as I woke up the following morning because I didn't actually wake up at all – not in the traditional sense. After falling asleep, extremely drunk, at around 2am, the very next thing I remember was finding myself right back on the ward in the nurses' office.

There was no moment where I was aware of waking up – it all happened instantaneously. I wasn't lying down or snoozing in a chair. I simply materialised in midstride, walking across the room holding a cup of coffee. I was also stone-cold sober, without even a hint of a hangover. That was impossible considering the amount I had imbibed over the previous two evenings.

Was my adventure over before it had even begun? Or had I imagined it all, after all? It seemed like I was back where I had started. If that was the case, why was I here and not in Thomas's room?

I looked across at the clock on the wall – a simple, white, plastic analogue clock which showed the time to be exactly 3am. That was more or less the time, by my reckoning, that I had originally left after the incident in Thomas's room.

The office, shared by all the nurses on shift, was cluttered with bags, food and other personal belongings that had been left lying around. My eye was drawn to a copy of *The Sun* on the desk which had been left there by one of the other nurses.

It wasn't my favourite rag, but now I seized it eagerly. Ignoring the headline about a Cabinet minister being caught watching lesbian porn on her smartphone during Prime Minister's Question Time, I scanned the top of the paper, searching for the date.

Friday 30th December 2022

Unless this paper had been left lying around in the office for months or years, it seemed that I hadn't returned to where I started at all. Instead, I was another whole year back in the past.

I examined the paper closely. It didn't look old or yellowed as papers did after a year or two. It looked as freshly minted as you would expect the current day's paper to look.

I remembered that story from the front page, too. The Minister had been forced to resign. That had indeed been a couple of years ago. If I was in any lingering doubts that I had gone back another year, they were soon squashed when the door opened, and the sister on duty that night walked in.

"Amy, we're just had someone brought up from A&E who was brought in after a cardiac arrest. Can you go and attend to his medication?"

Her actual words didn't really register, due to my surprise at seeing and hearing her again. The middle-aged, grey-haired lady in front of me was my mentor of many years, Sister Mary Williams. She had retired from the hospital and gone to live in Australia eighteen months ago. By that, I mean eighteen months ago from where I had started from, which from two years in the past meant about six months from now.

Her presence fitted in perfectly with what the date on the paper was telling me; even so, it had still come as a surprise and I was momentarily distracted thinking about the implications.

"Amy – did you hear what I said?" asked Sister Mary impatiently.

"Sorry, Sister," I replied, aware that I hadn't responded to her request. "I was miles away then. I'll get right onto it."

I tried to focus and recall exactly what she had said. Something about a heart attack victim and medication.

Before thinking, I inadvertently blurted out, "And it's great to see you again."

"You only saw me ten minutes ago," she replied, looking bemused.

Mary was a strict but kind woman and had taught me more about nursing than just about everyone else in the hospital put together. It was good to see her again. I almost wanted to hug her, but that would have been seriously weird from her perspective, where presumably everything seemed completely normal.

Instead, I took the details of the patient from her, made my way out of the room and got on with attending to my duties.

It wasn't easy to concentrate on what I was doing, consumed as I was with thoughts about this latest shift through time, and I had to force myself to be professional. I couldn't afford to screw up the medication for a heart attack patient with sky-high blood pressure.

He pretty much fitted the mould of our average cardiac patient – mid-fifties overweight boozers who never went to the doctors. We got them under control and sent them home with a load of pills and instructions to change their lifestyles.

Whether they did or not was up to them. As I attended to him, I tried to banish thoughts of time travel from my mind, but I simply could not help mulling over the enormity and uncertainty of the situation I was in.

The more I thought about it, the more tired I felt. Was my fatigue down to my recent experiences, or was it just because of my body's natural resistance to working nights? Perhaps it was both – an unwelcome mix of mental and physical exhaustion.

When my shift finished, I went straight home and slept, knowing that I was due in again in the evening for another stint. I wasn't sure if I was even going to go. With everything that was going on, I really needed a break from work.

When I woke, it was mid-afternoon and all was quiet in the flat. I had passed Phoebe and Lily in the morning while they were getting ready for their day shifts. We were often like this, ships passing in the night. Their absence from the flat gave me a chance to properly think about things, now that I had had a few hours of rejuvenating shut-eye.

To try and clarify everything, I jotted down on a notepad all the details I could remember from my journey so far. I knew that on my first jump through time, I had gone back from the early hours of 2nd January 2025 to sometime in the early morning of 31st December 2023. That was a year and two days.

I then stayed in that time zone for two further days before jumping back in time again. As far as I could ascertain, this had happened at roughly the same date and time as before. The crucial time seemed to be 3am on the 2nd of January. I couldn't be absolutely sure it was the exact time the second time around, as I had been asleep, but it had certainly been 3am when I had arrived in 2022.

It seemed that on my second trip back through time I had jumped back exactly the same amount as the first time, one year and two days.

There was an obvious pattern emerging here. It seemed that 3am on 2nd January was the trigger point for my involuntary trips back in time. The burning question for me now was whether or not that was the end of it. Would I stay put now, or was the pattern set to repeat? And if so, what were the implications?

If I kept jumping back in time like this every two days, I was going to travel further and further back into time, presumably getting younger as I did. I still wasn't entirely certain if it was just my mind that was being transported or my body as well, but I would find out soon enough if the jumps continued. After a few trips, if my body was getting younger, I would surely start to notice.

Being younger again was something that millions wished for, but I could already see that my fountain of youth was potentially a poisoned chalice. If I was going to get a year younger every two days, my life would fly by in no time.

I had been thirty-nine when all of this had started. At two days per leap, it would be less than eighty days until I would reach a time before I was born. So what would happen then? Would I just cease to exist?

What about my own birth? It was an event no human could remember under normal circumstances, but was I to experience it all, fully conscious with my adult mind, knowing I was living my last two days on earth?

Or would my immature and undeveloped brain no longer be able to make sense of all of this? Was I destined to end up a helpless infant, with no control over my bowels or bladder, like an incontinent, senile old person in reverse? The thought horrified me.

Was there any way out of this? Was there anyone who could help me? If I could track down the mysterious Doctor Gardner, perhaps he could, but I had no idea where to start. I didn't know his first name and I didn't even know if Gardner was his real name. He had been pretending to be a doctor, so had he used a false name as well?

Whoever he was, was he even aware of what he had done to me? I cursed the man and his time-travelling wand. Why had he let me get dragged into whatever he was up to? Didn't time travellers have rules about this sort of thing? They always did in the movies.

Assuming I wasn't going to find him, then what else was I to do? Wallow in self-pity or make the most of the time I had? I had to try and be positive. Maybe I did have less than eighty days left to live, but potentially they were full of opportunities.

49

I may have hated most of my birthdays the first time around but now they were positively sparkling with possibilities.

I pondered what was to happen in my new life as the years passed. Right now, here I was living with Phoebe and Lily, but in another couple of years that would come to an end and I'd never see them again.

Then there would be Rob. The man I had lived with for nine years who had betrayed me, belittled me and cheated on me. In return, I wasted the best years of my life on him. How was I going to be able to bear spending nine birthdays living with him?

Don't get mad – get even, whispered a voice inside my head.

It was an interesting thought. A woman scorned, getting her revenge in first? That could be a lot of fun.

In the years before I had saddled myself with Rob there had been college, travel, teenage crushes and more. The thoughts of those years excited me. Was this death sentence really so bad? How many with lives going nowhere would swap shoes with me, given the chance?

And what about the people I had lost – my mother, my father and especially my sister? Maybe I could help things turn out differently for them. Even if I couldn't, at least I would get to see them again and that was almost worth the cost of all this alone.

I decided to banish all thoughts of my impending mortality and seize the day. The possibilities were endless. I had no idea how all of this might end up playing out or what part I was going to play in it all, but it was time to start thinking ahead – or technically behind.

I needed to be sure I was going to jump again before I started making any plans that I might not be able to bring to fruition. So in the short term, it seemed best if I just played out the next two days as if life was proceeding just like normal. I would go to work like the dutiful soul I am, and then see if the jump back in time happened again on 2nd January.

If it did – then I would know that this was definitely game on. It was a game where I could tear up the rule book of life and throw it out of the window. There were new rules now, and I was seemingly the only one who knew what they were. That gave me an advantage over everyone else and a certain sense of power. The possibilities were thrilling. The world was about to become my own personal playground where I could do pretty much anything. Would this be abusing the gift I had seemingly been given? Very probably, but right at this time, I really didn't care.

I had nothing to lose and life was about to get all kinds of fun.

Chapter Five
2021

I had stayed up until 3am because I wanted to be wide awake when the jump happened. When it did, the last thing I remember was looking at the digital clock in my room as it ticked over to precisely 3am. The next thing I knew, I was waking up and it was 8.30am in the morning.

This didn't mean I had arrived at that time. I was pretty sure it meant I had arrived at 3am as before but had been asleep in this body at that time. That was to be expected – if I wasn't at work I would almost certainly be asleep at that time as most people, party animals aside, would be.

I went straight for my phone, which I noticed was now an S10, for the confirmation I sought. It was 31st December 2021, just as I had expected. That settled it, then. The pattern was clear. I was travelling back a year and two days in time every forty-eight hours, as regular as clockwork. Except I was living by a clock unlike any that had ever been invented.

Seemingly it was only me that this was happening to. Everyone else I had seen or spoken to in the last few days had been acting completely normally. I think if the whole world was being cast back in time simultaneously it would have been pretty obvious – and probably extremely chaotic.

I sat up in bed, once again contemplating my situation, as I had so many times in previous days. Last night I had felt quite excited by my newfound ability to travel in time, but would I carry on with this if I had a choice? I had to be honest and admit I wouldn't. I would stop this right now if I could. But what could I possibly do?

It seemed that I would have to assume that there was no way to stop it, so perhaps I ought to accept the situation and start thinking about what I should be doing with my time.

I likened my position to someone with a terminal illness who had just been told they had less than three months to live. That was effectively my life expectancy. I had already done the calculations.

Perhaps that was looking at it from a somewhat pessimistic angle. I wasn't dying of a terminal illness. Yes, my days were numbered, but the potential those days held was enormous. I wasn't going to get sick and spend a large chunk of my final days dosed up on morphine in a hospice with everyone feeling sorry for me.

I was going to get younger, having discovered that fountain of youth that had eluded everyone from ancient alchemists to the most advanced modern scientists. I was going to get a chance to relive snapshots from my past all over again, including seeing long-lost loved ones again. This was an amazing gift that had been bestowed upon me and seemingly me alone.

If I was to be stuck in reverse gear, then what consequences would any actions I took in the past have? If I was destined to keep travelling back every two days, then would each trip back absolve me from any actions I might take? Had I been given free rein to do whatever I wanted? – even a licence to kill, should I so desire. What better place could there be to hide from such a crime than in the past, before it had even happened?

A fleeting dark thought crossed my mind as I thought about stabbing Rob to death with a kitchen knife in a wanton and unrestrained act of revenge for his infidelity. It wasn't the first time I had fantasised about doing him in.

For all I knew maybe everyone thought such things from time to time, but very few ever acted upon these deep, dark impulses. Even if they did possess the balls to do it, a life sentence in prison was deterrent enough for most. But that wasn't something that I needed to worry about anymore.

I could kill Rob, then jump back in time a year before the police could track me down. And even if they did catch me in the act, all I needed to do was ride out my time in custody until the next jump back in time came round at which point I would automatically escape.

Then I could kill him all over again. And then again – every one of the nine years we had been together. He would be like a cat with nine lives, and I could end every one of them, despatching him in a grisly variety of different ways. I could be the ultimate serial killer, with the twist that my nine murders would all be of the same man and the police would never be able to catch up with me. What a plot for a thriller that would make!

Much as I was revelling in this fantasy, it wasn't one I had any real intention of carrying out. Quite simply, it all boiled down to the truth that I wasn't a killer and never could be. I just didn't have it in me and I was thankful about that.

It didn't mean there weren't lots of other non-lethal ways I could get back at him, though. I smiled as I toyed with various possibilities.

Other than making Rob's life a misery, what else could I do? I needed to have a good review of my own personal history and start making some plans. Could I figure out exactly what I was doing in each individual year?

There were landmark events during certain years that stood out, but what about all those other nondescript New Year's Eves and birthdays? They all blurred into one and I couldn't honestly pinpoint which year was which in the random snippets of my memories.

The short answer was no. I couldn't do it from memory alone. I was going to have to play detective with my own life, using social media and anything else I could to try and pinpoint what I was going to be doing each year.

Eager to get started on embracing my new life, I climbed out of bed and headed over to the window to open the curtains. Then I made a beeline for my bag, which had seemingly been discarded on the other side of the room when I had got in from whatever this version of me had been doing last night.

Each time I went back in time I noticed subtle changes all around me, and this bag was a prime example. It was my old bag which I'd had five or six good years' use out of before the strap had broken.

I had really loved this bag. It was black with a variety of leaves on it, in various shades of autumn colour. Although pretty, the exterior wasn't the most important factor when I had bought it. The biggest-selling point for me was that it had pockets everywhere – and pockets are awesome.

This bag had them on the inside, outside, in hidden flaps, with zips and buttons everywhere. In total, there were fourteen pockets and every one had its own little function – right down to my emergency condom pocket. It was hidden by a tiny zip just enough to hold a single Durex in case I got lucky unexpectedly.

I seldom did, but it was best to be prepared, even if in recent years, in the heat of the moment, I hadn't always been as careful as I should have been. Perhaps that was down to the biological clock, too. Tick-tock… and then pregnant by a one-night stand and a single mum at my age? It wasn't that unheard of. By accidentally on purpose forgetting to ask my partner to rubber up, was I subconsciously fulfilling some primaeval desire to get pregnant?

This hadn't happened in my case, which was probably just as well considering my current situation. If I had had a baby in the last couple of years, how heart-wrenching would it be to be parted from him or her by my backwards time-travelling? I couldn't even begin to imagine, not having been a mother myself.

Rediscovering my bag instilled a real sense of nostalgia in me. Temporarily forgetting why I had picked it up in the first place, I put it down on the bed and cast my eyes around the room, looking for more changes. Seeing some discarded garments of yesteryear scattered around prompted me to get up and open the wardrobe. Looking inside, I found much of that had changed, too.

What about myself? Taking out an old rugby-style shirt I used to wear on days when I was bumming around the flat, I closed the door again and took a good look at myself in the mirror.

Did I look any younger compared to when this started? It was hard to tell. How much did people change in three years? Perhaps they did not change much in their thirties because I still couldn't make out any discernible differences. If I was Lily it would have been obvious from the ever-changing hairstyles, and presence or otherwise of tattoos, but I had none.

I cupped my breasts in my hands – was it my imagination or did they feel a little firmer? Once I had taken a few more years off they would rival Phoebe's for defying gravity, but then in those few years I would have no Phoebe to compare against – because she wouldn't have arrived in my life yet.

2021 was the year we had all moved into the flat so this would be our last two days together. I felt a pang of impending loss wash over me about this. It was something I was going to have to get used to. People were going to come in and out of my life pretty rapidly in the weeks ahead and I have to make the most of whatever time I had with the people who mattered to me.

For the next two days that meant Phoebe and Lily, and this realisation reminded me of why I had gone for the bag in the first place. It was so easy to get distracted with all the diversions my new life had brought Turning my attention back to the matter in hand, I reached into one of the many pockets on the inside of my bag to retrieve my work diary.

That was another thing that would change each year. This diary had a picture of ladybirds and butterflies on it. It was just a cheap, pound shop diary, but I bought most things like that from those sorts of places. I couldn't see the point of spending four quid on something that was practically identical from WHSmith.

The diary looked brand new so it must have been for the year ahead, not the one just ending. Hopefully, I had started filling it in already. Thumbing through to find the first week, I discovered that it actually began from the start of the current week, five days ago, and all my shifts were neatly written in.

It came as no surprise to discover I was pencilled in to be working nights again over New Year, starting from tonight. Well, it was time to take an executive decision – there was no way I was going in to work tonight – or any other night, come to that. The expression "life's too short" had never been more apt than it was for me right now.

Yes, I was conscientious about my work, but only up to a point. Not turning up tonight wasn't going to affect my non-existent future in this world.

I didn't want to leave the hospital in the lurch, though, and did feel a certain responsibility to whatever patients might be counting on a fully staffed ward. Whatever the shortcomings of the NHS might be, I didn't want to be the one to let the patients down, so as a compromise, I decided I would phone in sick. That would give them time to arrange some cover for me. Then I would go out with Phoebe and Lily to get sloshed and have a good time.

Speaking of my flatmates, just as I was formulating these plans I heard an annoyed shout from the kitchen.

"Hey, Phoebe – did you use all the milk?"

I was so going to miss these two. Eagerly I pulled on the rugby shirt and headed out into the flat, clad in just that and my knickers. I heard the welcome rumble of the coffee percolator on the go which meant that Lily was preparing her daily caffeine fix and I wanted in.

Sure enough, there she was in the kitchen. Her hair had changed again. There were no dreads now, just long, straight hair which was dyed a brilliant purple. And she certainly looked much younger than before.

"Ugh – too much flesh, pet," was her first remark on clocking my scantily clad lower regions. "You're getting as bad as Phoebe – go and get some clothes on."

"What is it with you and naked flesh?" I asked playfully.

"I don't mind it on a fella," replied Lily, "but I'm not into girls – even though the way everyone goes on about it you would think we were all bisexual these days."

I laughed and replied, "No worries, I'll go and stick my dressing gown on. By the way – what are you up to tonight?"

"We've got tickets for *Fever*, remember?" she replied. "It's going to be awesome. I wish you were coming."

"Well, you're in luck – because I am," I replied.

"I thought you were supposed to be working?" she queried.

"Not anymore," I replied. "I managed to swap a shift. So the three amigos can ride again!"

"Cool," said Lily. "I assume you've got a ticket, then? Because when you said you weren't coming, I did only get the two for me and Phoebe – and they were hard enough to come by."

I hadn't got a ticket. But that wasn't going to stop me from getting one. This was an opportunity to make the most of my altered circumstances to disregard the normal rules and push the boat out.

"How much did you pay for them?" I asked.

"£25 each," she replied. "But they won't have any left now – they sold out weeks ago."

"Everyone has their price." I grinned. "I'll get one – you'll see."

I poured myself a coffee from the large pot that Lily had brewed.

"You'll have to use Coffee-mate," said Lily. "Phoebe's had all the milk again."

"That's not a problem," I said. "I like Coffee-mate."

"I don't," replied Lily. "But it looks like I'm going to have to make do with it because Miss Piggy's in the shower and I can't face going out to the shop without having a coffee first."

I could hear the shower going. It had been on the whole time I had been in the kitchen.

"Looks like she's using all the hot water as well," I remarked.

"Will you go and tell her, pet, because last time I went in there I caught her masturbating with the shower head and it's not something I want to see again," said Lily, with a disgusted look on her face.

"Don't you ever…umm, you know?" I asked.

"Maybe I do, but if so it's in the privacy of my own room when everyone's out," she replied.

As she spoke, the sound of the shower shut off, sparing either of us from walking in on whatever Phoebe had been up to. Instead, Lily returned to our earlier topic of conversation.

"How are you going to get this ticket, then?" she asked.

"Piece of cake," I said as I headed back to the bedroom, coffee in hand. I had already figured out what I was going to do and wanted to get started.

Pulling out my phone, I got straight onto the Oxford For Sale/Wanted page on Facebook where I posted this.

WANTED: New Year's Eve ticket for Fever in Oxford tonight. Willing to pay £100 cash. PM me for details.

There is no way I would normally have paid that sort of money just to get into a nightclub, but the old restrictions no longer applied. If I was only going to be here for forty-eight hours, then money no longer had any meaning for me. I could spend to my heart's content. The sky was the limit. Well, five grand was about the actual limit, which was what I could run up on my credit card.

That was a lot of spending money for two days and the beauty of it was, I'd never have to pay any of it off. As soon as I jumped back in time, the slate would be wiped clean and I could start spending all over again. Just like when I was fantasising about murdering Rob: there were no consequences.

While I was waiting for the replies to flood in, I rang in sick to work, hoping it wouldn't be Sister Mary who answered. She would give me a right rollicking for calling in sick at New Year, even if I was dying. Technically I was, but not in a way I could explain to her.

Fortunately, I got Tessa instead, so I put on my best sick person voice and bleated pathetically into the phone as I pretended to have flu.

She seemed to believe me, advising me to wrap up warm and go back to bed, so I thanked her and hung up. Then I turned my attention back to Facebook to discover three people had already messaged me with offers of tickets.

Two of the respondents were male and I didn't like the look of either of them from their profile pictures. I don't know exactly what it was, but they just looked dodgy, more like police mugshots than social media-friendly portraits.

Trusting my gut feelings, I ignored them because as soon as I saw the third thumbnail, my eyes were drawn instinctively towards it. It was of a girl called Kacey who looked vaguely familiar. I felt as if I knew her, but I couldn't remember where from to begin with.

I read through her message which described a seemingly genuine enough reason for not going out – she had been let down by her babysitter. She lived close by, just two streets away which was a bonus. I wouldn't have to go far out of my way to acquire the ticket.

I looked closely at her picture again. Where did I know that girl from? It was bugging me so I went to have a snoop around her profile. As soon as I enlarged her profile picture to full size, it clicked.

She was the single mother I had comforted in hospital after taking an overdose when her kid had been taken into care. Or rather, she would be. All of that was three years from now and there was no indication in this happy, healthy photo of the traumas that lay ahead.

That settled it – I would definitely be buying the ticket from her, and she would be getting more than just money for it.

I needed to have a serious talk with her. Other than fantasising about murdering my ex-boyfriend I had been wondering what else I could do with my spontaneous trips back through time. Now it seemed I had been handed a cast-iron opportunity to be a Good Samaritan.

I messaged Kacey back and arranged to call round to her place. She sounded thrilled in her reply – and who wouldn't be in her position? A hundred pounds would go a long way for a single mother.

Dressing quickly, I headed back into the main part of the flat.

"Nailed it," I said triumphantly to Lily, who was still moping around in the kitchen, coffee cup in hand.

"How much did you pay for it?" she asked.

"Oh, enough," I replied vaguely. I didn't want to tell her exactly how much. She would have thought I was crazy and would want to know why.

Skipping breakfast for the moment, I stopped briefly in the bathroom, thankfully now Phoebe-free, to clean my teeth and put the shower head back on its holder. I tried not to think about the likely reason it had been left dangling over the taps. Then I headed out, a girl on a mission.

My first stop was the cashpoint where I drew out the maximum allowed on my debit card – £500. From a financial perspective, the timing of my trips back in time couldn't be better. Not only had I just been paid, as it was the end of the month, but also my rent didn't go out until the 3rd of January. By that time I'd be long gone. And of course, I had a credit card, too. This all added up to make me a woman of significant means.

I walked through Headington, along a street that had a famous house with a shark sticking out of its roof, heading for

Kacey's flat. As I strolled along I tried to work out what I was going to say to her. I couldn't think of any way of putting it that wouldn't sound weird, so I would just have to go for it and hope that my message would sink in.

Her flat was on the ground floor of a recently built social housing block. Despite only being a couple of years old, it already looked grubby. There was no shortage of litter blowing around the communal bins outside. A rough-looking character in a red hoodie was sitting on an expensive-looking mountain bike next to the bins, blatantly talking into his phone about a pick-up which could mean only one thing. Fortunately, he ignored me, so I pressed the button for her flat and she buzzed me in.

The shared hallway stank of dope. From what little I had seen of this area already, it didn't surprise me at all that she had fallen into the clutches of this Aaron character. Maybe that had even been him outside.

I knocked on the door, and she answered, baby girl clutched to her breast.

"Hi – Kacey?" I said, in that questioning way people do just to reassure themselves that they've got the right person. "I've come for the ticket."

"Come in," she said. "I'm just finishing feeding the baby – you don't mind, do you?"

"Of course not," I said, and I followed her into the kitchen area of the tiny flat. She put the baby over her shoulder, patted her back and put her down into a small playpen where she lay, smiling and gurgling, on her back. I guessed she must have been about three or four months old.

"I couldn't believe it when I saw your post," said Kacey. "I was gutted when Mum said she couldn't babysit, but her new boyfriend's taking her out."

63

As she spoke, I was struck by how different this girl was from the train wreck I was to encounter at the hospital three years in the future.

She was bubbly, bright and clean. Not only that, the flat, despite her having a baby, was also clean and tidy. I always felt you could tell a lot from a person's home. If they kept that in good order, it was likely their lives would be, too.

I found it disturbing, having the foreknowledge of how far she would fall in such a short time. Seeing her like this made me ever more determined to make her listen. If ever there was a case of prevention being better than cure, surely this was it.

She was still talking as these thoughts were going through my head.

"David – that's my mum's boyfriend – he said this was a con and no one would pay a hundred pounds for a ticket," she continued.

"Don't worry, it's not a con," I reassured her. "I've got the money right here." I pulled out my purse and patted it. "But a cup of coffee and a chat would be nice if you can stretch to that?"

"I'd love that," she said. "You wouldn't believe how bored and lonely I get stuck at home on my own all the time. Yes, I get to go out to mother and baby groups and stuff, but it's all baby talk there, you know?"

I didn't know, but I could imagine. In the interest of winning her trust, I nodded my agreement.

"The evenings are the worst. Once Maddie goes down for the evening it's just me and the TV." She paused and then added. "Do you have kids?"

Should I lie? No – I might get tripped up by it. Best to be honest.

"No," I replied. "I've never quite got round to it."

"Not found the right man, yet, eh?" she asked.

"Something like that," I replied, not really wanting to get into the whole Rob thing.

"I thought I had," she said. "My ex – Steven. At least until I got pregnant. Then it all started to go wrong. He dumped me about two weeks before the baby was due. Said he wasn't ready to be a dad and I haven't seen him since."

"I'm sorry," I said, which is pretty much my default response to being told anything like this. I can never think of anything else to say.

"Don't be," she said. "He was a waste of space. Just after I told him I was pregnant he gave up his job because he said he was going to become an artist. When that didn't happen, he said he couldn't support a child and that was the end of it. Next time I'm going to get myself a man with a bit more about him."

Which I knew was going to be very bad news and the very thing I had come here to warn her about. Her last sentence had given me the perfect lead-in for what I had come here to say.

"Yeah, about that," I replied. "I'll come clean with you – I did have an ulterior motive for coming here today."

"I knew it," she said, her face falling. "David said this was too good to be true. Did Steven send you? Because if he did, then you can tell him it's too late. I don't want anything more to do with him."

"Relax," I said. Keen to reassure her, I opened my purse, counted out five twenty-pound notes and handed them to her.

"There," I said. "It's not a scam and don't worry. I've never met Steven."

She passed the ticket over to me, and I tucked it back in my wallet. Business concluded, it was now time for the tricky bit.

"Thank you," she said. "This money is going to come in very handy. You wouldn't believe how many things you need for a baby."

"So, I guess you're wondering why else I'm here," I said. "I do need to give you a message, but it's not from Steven."

"Who from, then?" she said, looking intrigued.

Here goes, I thought. It's now or never.

"From the future," I declared, possibly slightly overdramatically.

"Really?" she said, raising her eyebrows. It was clear she wasn't taking this seriously, but had I honestly expected her to?

"Look, just hear me out," I said. Whatever I was going to say, I had to get it across quickly before she dismissed me as some madwoman. There was no time for any long-winded explanation. I just had to spit it out.

"I've come here from three years in the future where you're lying in a hospital bed. You're a junkie who has taken an overdose."

"I've never taken drugs in my life," she protested, a look of disbelief, not to mention a little anger, on her face.

"And I hope you never will," I said. Pressing on, I added, "It all depends on what you do this year."

She opened her mouth as if to protest further but I cut her off.

"Just listen. Later on this year, you are going to meet a guy called Aaron. You're going to think he's the bee's knees and fall hook, line and sinker for him. You won't see what he's really like until it's too late. The reality is, whatever charm he spins you, he's a drug dealer, a bully and he'll abuse you so badly you'll be driven to try to take your own life."

She looked at me, a look of horror on her face, still tinged with disbelief, but there was no doubt I had her attention.

"Oh, and there's one final thing. You see that beautiful baby over there?" I gestured over to where the baby was now asleep in her pen. "You're going to lose her, too."

"Who the hell are you?" she reacted angrily, eyes blazing, but with a hint of tears behind them. "What do you think you're doing, coming here scaring me like this?"

"Look, just trust me. I know your future and you don't have one worth living if you get together with this Aaron."

"I don't even know anyone called Aaron," she insisted. "You'd better leave, right now."

She got up and began to usher me towards the door.

"Look, you don't have to believe me right now, but just remember what I've said. If someone called Aaron comes into your life, keep away from him. Or at least do your homework – find out about him before you get involved. Seriously, your whole future depends on it."

"You're insane! Just get out!" she yelled, pushing me through the door, and slamming it behind me. From the other side, I could hear the sound of sobbing.

Had I done the right thing? Would she remember what I'd said? Had I achieved anything here today at all, other than to upset a vulnerable young woman? I had no way of finding out the answers to any of these questions. All I could hope was that by being cruel, I had ultimately been kind.

When I went back outside, the dodgy geezer I'd seen before was still out there, dialling a number on his phone. As I passed him, I caught the start of the conversation.

"Dale, it's Aaron. I'm in the new flat, mate, just moved in last night. The coast's clear if you wanna bring the stuff over."

It had to be him: it couldn't just be a coincidence. Sure, there was more than one Aaron in the world, but somehow I just knew this was the guy. It all fitted.

He glanced at me briefly as I passed with a look of distaste on his face. He really did look like a nasty piece of work, but I could see why Kacey could be taken in by him. He was a bad boy, but a good-looking bad boy, and they were the most dangerous ones of all.

Seeing him had given me an idea. Maybe there was something else I could do. I headed round the corner, well out of earshot, and then dialled 101 on my mobile. When I got through, I gave the police a good description of Aaron and told them I'd just seen him dealing drugs outside the flats.

They said they would send someone down to investigate. I had my doubts about whether it would do any good because the likes of Aaron seemed to have a talent for staying one step ahead of the police.

Perhaps they would get lucky, catch him in possession and then Kacey might be spared the misfortune of ever meeting him. Failing that, hopefully, she would take heed of my warning and make a different choice when the time came.

Would she? I wasn't sure. I had seen so many friends over the years make unsuitable choices because they kept their brains in their knickers when it came to men. And if I was totally honest, I had been guilty of it myself on more than one occasion. Fortunately, the worst that had happened to me was being cheated on – I hadn't been abused or bullied like Kacey would be if she didn't give this guy a wide berth.

I had done all I possibly could. It was out of my hands now and time to get on with the rest of my plans for the day.

I was done here.

Chapter Six
2021

With my newly acquired *Fever* ticket safely stowed away in my bag, I walked into the centre of Headington towards the bus stop.

At least a dozen people were waiting, including three young mothers with pushchairs, all jockeying for pole position at the front. They knew the buses only had room for two pushchairs and one was going to have to fold theirs up and have their baby on their lap. That was assuming, of course, that when the bus came, the spots weren't already taken.

I watched as the mothers eyeballed each other, determined not to be the one to cede territory. The longer it took for the bus to come, the more full it was likely to be. When it would come was another matter.

I looked up at the electronic board inside the bus shelter. It was displaying the information that bus number nine was due which wasn't very helpful as there was no sign of it – not in the direction I wanted to go anyway. On the other side of the road, two number nines swept past in convoy, bound for Barton. I had never had much luck with the buses in Oxford.

Then a thought struck me – why waste my now precious time hanging around for a bus? There was a taxi rank just up from the bus stop, so I went and hopped in the back of the one at the front of the queue, a white Toyota Prius.

The interior had a sickly sweet smell coming from a collection of dangling Christmas tree-shaped air fresheners in the front. It wasn't quite enough to hide the stench of stale cigar smoke coming from the driver, a fat, middle-aged man who looked like he probably needed to be winched in and out of the cab.

I sank back on the soft, black leather seats, buckled up and said, "Town please."

I got a grunt of acknowledgement and that amounted to the sum total of our conversation all the way into the city centre. So much for taxi drivers being talkative and friendly – this one certainly wasn't getting a tip even if I was now a woman of considerable means.

Travelling by taxi was a rarity for me. I am of a frugal nature, brought on by years of being a poor student followed by years more of trying to make ends meet on a nurse's salary in Oxford. I considered taxis to be an unnecessary luxury. If there was a bus available, I took it, even if that bus happened to be the last one home at 2am, full of annoying drunks and people eating stinky takeaways.

With my newfound spending power, it was quite exhilarating to be able to cast off the shackles of austerity. This taxi was the second thing I had splashed out on today, and I wasn't finished yet. The purse strings had been slashed wide open and I already had my next purchase in mind.

The taxi dropped me opposite the entrance to the Covered Market on the High Street. I paid the driver, eliciting another barely audible grunt in response, and headed across the road, hoping that what I had come for was still here.

I had recalled during my taxi ride that two or three years ago, Phoebe and I had come Christmas shopping together. We had walked through the market looking at all the seasonal displays from the many and varied retailers inside, mostly goods we couldn't afford.

Christmas shopping wasn't something I did much of these days – with most of my family dead I had very few people to buy for. But Phoebe insisted I come with her, as Lily had been working, so off to town we went – on the bus, naturally.

On that day we had been wandering along one of the narrow passages that made up this historic rabbit warren of a market when I had spotted a gorgeous dress in the window of a recently opened boutique. When I pointed it out to Phoebe she encouraged me to try it on, which I did – and even I was stunned at the outcome.

Generally, I am terrible when it comes to clothes shopping. Everything that looks amazing on a shop window dummy looks like it's just been draped over the branches of a tree when it's put on me. Or that's what I think, anyway.

Shop assistants tend to be more enthusiastic, but since most of them are on commission I take all that "it looks lovely on you" stuff with a pinch of salt. At least with Phoebe in tow, I was able to get an unbiased second opinion.

Early in our relationship, I managed to get Rob to come with me clothes shopping a few times, but he had been no help. It was quite clear from all the eye-rolling and grumbling that he would far rather be elsewhere.

Perhaps I should have taken that as a warning sign of what was to come. Doubtless, he felt the same on the rare occasions we were having sex once he had Emma next door. He had probably been fantasising about her while we were doing it.

I certainly couldn't trust him to give me an unbiased opinion on any clothes I tried on. Usually, he would say anything looked good to get me to buy it so we could get out of the shop and go to the pub. I could have draped a bin liner over myself and he would have said it looked good. In the end, I stopped asking him to accompany me.

Shopping with girlfriends was different: they never seemed to get bored. Their reactions were genuine and I knew from the way Phoebe had enthused about this slinky little red number that I'd found the perfect dress.

It doesn't happen very often, especially if you are as fussy as me. Such moments come along once or twice a lifetime at best. I knew right then that I had to have it.

That was before I looked at the price tag and discovered that I couldn't have it. £499.99 was out of my price range by at least £400 so I reluctantly gave the dress back to the assistant and left, feeling pretty crestfallen. I was so downhearted that it took three pints with Phoebe in The Chequers over the road to quell the disappointment.

I hadn't forgotten about that dress and it had come up in conversation a few times since.

"Remember that gorgeous dress you found in the market that time?" Phoebe would say.

"Don't remind me," I'd reply, wishing just once that I could have one of the finer things in life for myself.

Now here I was, back in the past and keeping my fingers crossed that this was that same year Phoebe and I had gone Christmas shopping and that if it was, the dress was still there. That shopping trip had been a week before Christmas and it was two weeks later now, so even if it was the right year, someone else might have grabbed it by now.

Fortunately, I was right on both counts. It was the right year and it was still there, sitting in the window just as I remembered. As a bonus, it was now reduced in the New Year sale to £249.99, not that that made one iota of a difference. Nothing was going to stop me from buying it this time and I would have paid double the original price if I'd had to.

I went in and tried it on again, just to be sure. It was a red satin skater dress which hugged my hips perfectly before billowing out in an A shape to just above my knees. It was also very flattering for my boobs – with this on I would have a bust to almost rival Phoebe's, and that was saying something.

I paid the £250 using my credit card, a twinge of naughtiness seeping through me as I typed in my PIN. It felt like I was doing something I shouldn't be, almost akin to stealing. But who was I stealing from – the credit card company? My future self? It was a rather grey area.

I was half-expecting the card to be declined as if someone somewhere knew what I was up to, but my fears were unfounded. The transaction went through perfectly and I finally owned my dream dress. Now all I needed was a pair of shoes to go with it.

To say I got carried away with my shopping would be somewhat of an understatement. It was already dark when I got back to the flat, via a taxi, naturally, with almost a grand's worth of goods in tow. Phoebe and Lily were both in the flat watching TV, but I managed to sneak past them into my room without them seeing just how many bags I had. I wanted to surprise them.

I jumped in the shower while I had the chance, came back into the kitchen in my dressing gown to grab a bite to eat and then retired to my room to get ready. At 7pm, I emerged, excitedly wearing my dream dress.

Lily and Phoebe were in the kitchen. They were both in their party outfits by now and making serious inroads into a bottle of white wine.

"Oh my God, you look amazing," said Lily.

"Wow – the dress from the market! I can't believe you got it!" exclaimed Phoebe. "How did you afford it?"

"New Year's sale," I said. "Let's just say it's an early birthday present," I added.

"I didn't know your birthday was coming up," said Lily. "When is it?"

Of course, they didn't know. That made sense as it was our first year together and I probably hadn't told them yet for all the usual reasons. But now seemed as good a time as any to let them know.

"Actually, it's tomorrow," I said.

"Oh my days!" exclaimed Phoebe. "I can't believe you didn't tell us! Big party tonight, then! Even bigger than it was already going to be!"

She reached into the cupboard and pulled out a whisky tumbler.

"Here – have a glass of wine," she said, emptying the remainder of the Chardonnay into it.

It was the wrong sort of glass, but we only had two wine glasses. Our kitchen was a complete mishmash of odd plates, cups and other bits of pieces we had all brought with us when we moved in. The same could be said of the whole flat, really. Any interior designer would have recoiled at it, but we liked it that way, random, haphazard and homely.

As I drank my wine, joining in the banter going on between us girlies, I realised I was really enjoying myself. Perhaps I was going to have to rethink my previous Scrooge-like attitude to New Year. Why had I been such a killjoy in the past?

I think I can answer my own question. Before it had been just humdrum real life, drifting along from one year to the next, but now I had a time limit. I had to live like there was no tomorrow because in my case, there literally wasn't. It was time to party hard.

Full of enthusiasm for the night ahead, the three of us grabbed a taxi – my treat – and headed out for the club, three excited young things off for a night of adventure. And in what was now my thirty-four-year-old body, I really did feel like a young person again and I was only going to get younger.

Despite starting with what might have been unrealistically high hopes, the night didn't disappoint. I took full advantage of my situation to make it one of the best ever. With all inhibitions cast aside, some twelve hours after we'd left for town, I found myself waking up with a simply gorgeous man by my side.

His name was Carl and he reminded me of a young Kiefer Sutherland from the early years of *24*. Fortunately, this man did not have such a dangerous lifestyle as Jack Bauer. He had some high-paid research post at the university. That's what he had told me anyway, as he was sweeping me off my feet at the bar shortly before midnight the previous evening.

A New Year's kiss inevitably followed, and three hours after that we were at it like rabbits, not once, but twice. Now he was sleeping, but as I wriggled down the bed to wake him up in the most pleasant of ways, I was determined to go for the hat-trick.

It wasn't like me to jump into bed with someone on the night I met them – that was more Phoebe's thing, but if I hadn't done it last night, when would I do it? I could hardly ask him to meet me for a date a year in the past, could I? I had to grab him while I could so there was no way I was going to pass up an opportunity like this.

He was quite probably the most gorgeous man ever to show an interest in me. Just talking to him at the bar had given me what Phoebe rather crudely referred to as "the fanny gallops". I knew right there and then that I had to have him, but the night was still young at that point.

After a couple of hours more drinking and dancing, I naughtily suggested in his ear that he might like to come back for "coffee", meaning of course more than coffee. From the grin on his face, he certainly knew what I meant.

Leaving Phoebe and Lily still enjoying the party, I took him home in my third taxi of the day. Back at the flat, he proved to be an accomplished lover.

How had I managed to pull such a gorgeous man? I have no idea. Maybe it was the dress, or perhaps it was just my newfound devil-may-care persona. Either way, I wasn't complaining. What had I been missing out on all these years spending my New Years doing night shifts at the hospital?

After I'd had my wicked way with him a third time and we started to get dressed, he asked the question that under any other circumstances, I'd have been delighted to hear.

"I think you're awesome," he said. "Can I see you again?"

"Of course," I replied. "Give me a ring in a couple of days and maybe we could go out at the weekend." It was a hollow promise about a weekend I would never see. I'd never see this man again either, and that cut me up. Finally, I had met a decent one but in less than twenty-four hours I'd be spirited back into the past and that would be the end of it.

It would be the end of it for me, anyway, but what about him? My mind might be heading back through time, but what about the body that was here – the "me" that was here before? Would I/she carry on as if nothing had happened? Would she remember any of this? It wasn't the first time I had asked myself this question and it intrigued me.

It could be that this other self of mine might be able to start a relationship with this man. Had I made life different and better for that other me by doing what I had done? I don't know, but if it was a possibility, then by agreeing to see him again I was giving her every chance. Whether or not she'd be so pleased when the credit card bill arrived was another matter, but still, if she got the man of her dreams out of it, then it was all a solid investment, wasn't it?

I was hypothesising. I didn't know how all this worked. Maybe I never would, so perhaps I ought to tread carefully. I had been sure that I wouldn't have the guts to do anything really bad like killing Rob, which was probably a good thing. With the punishment of an alternate version of me a possibility, I couldn't risk it. I didn't want to condemn that possible other self to a lifetime in prison.

As far as this man went, if there was to be a relationship in this timeline, then it had started very promisingly, judging by his reply to my response suggesting meeting up at the weekend.

"I'd love that," he said, adding, "By the way, I really love your Liverpool accent." He sounded like he genuinely meant it, which I appreciated. This man was so amazing it almost made up for all those times being teased about my Scouse origins at school.

I was almost tempted to ask him for another date tonight while I had the chance but I held back. I could quite easily fall head over heels for Carl and that would only bring me heartbreak when we were forced to part and then that would be another New Year of woe. I needed to quit while I was ahead and besides, I had other plans.

After I showed him out, enjoying a final snog at the door, I went back into the flat and thought about what was to come. Lily and Phoebe were still in bed and I continued to mull over things as I put the coffee pot on.

It was my final day here. Not only would I not see Carl again, but also I wouldn't see this flat or Phoebe and Lily again. That made me sad. The fun I had just enjoyed was well and truly tinged with a melancholy edge.

Tomorrow I would be back in my old house with Rob. It wasn't something I was looking forward to, but I was going to make the most of the opportunity to make him pay for what he had done – hopefully in a way that wouldn't land me in trouble with the police. He had no idea what was coming his way.

In the meantime, it was high time I did something about trying to find a way out of my situation, in the unlikely event that a way out existed. If it did, I had to give myself every chance to find it.

I turned on my phone, noting that there were several missed calls from the hospital. I don't know what that was all about. Tessa should have told them that I had phoned in sick unless she was so busy scoffing mince pies she had forgotten.

Ignoring the calls, I went to Google and tried looking up Doctor Gardner and time travel. No luck there. Then I tried time travel and John Radcliffe Hospital which came up similarly fruitless.

I played around with a few more search terms until finally "Time Travel Oxford" produced an interesting result. It threw up the following magazine article.

Time travel is possible claims Oxford Professor.

I went on to read about Professor Antony Hamilton and his experiments into time travel at Oxford University. The article was dated three years previously, so I had plenty of time to track him down. I decided to make his college my first port of call on my next trip back through time.

I was interrupted by my phone ringing. It was the hospital again. This was getting irksome. What was so important it couldn't wait? Well, it would have to. I rejected the call and went back into the flat where Phoebe and Lily were now up and about.

"Ooh, here she is," cooed Phoebe. "We were wondering when you were going to surface, you mucky cow."

"Sounds like you enjoyed yourself last night," said Lily knowingly.

I blushed, replying, "Sorry, did you hear me?"

"I think the whole building did, pet," she replied. "I'm not used to hearing it through that wall. It's normally coming from the other side."

She nodded towards Phoebe as she spoke.

"Not last night," said Phoebe. "I can't believe you pulled and I didn't."

"Sorry," I said. "Am I that hideous, then?"

"Of course not," she said. "I didn't mean it like that." She looked worried that she might have offended me.

"It's cool, I'm just kidding," I replied, to set her mind at rest.

"I don't want to worry you," said Lily. "But Sister Mary's been trying to get hold of you. Something about pictures of you on the internet partying last night while you were supposed to be off sick. She's been sending me messages asking me where you are."

"Oh shit," I said, "I forgot about that."

We had been posting selfies all night on Facebook which was probably not the smartest thing to do when pulling a sickie. Never mind – it wasn't going to be my problem.

Sorry, other Amy, I thought to myself. *But at least you got a new boyfriend out of it.*

"Don't worry about it now, Amy, it's your birthday," said Phoebe. "Close your eyes and count to thirty. We've got something for you."

I complied, and when I opened them I was presented with another cake, thankfully not in the shape of a penis this time.

"Sorry it's only a Peppa Pig one," said Phoebe, "but you didn't tell us it was your birthday until yesterday so I didn't have time to make one. This was all they had left in the shop."

"It's lovely," I said. "Thank you."

"Make a wish," said Lily, as I blew out the single candle on my cake. In a few weeks, would I be trying pathetically to blow out a single candle with my one-year-old lungs? I don't mind admitting I was scared.

Cake devoured, we all went out and got drunk again. These last few days with Phoebe and Lily had been simply amazing.

I was so going to miss them.

Chapter Seven
2020

For the first time since all of this started, I arrived in my next time zone with some proper plans. Despite my drunken state on my last night with the girls, I had lain awake for the last hour or so of my time in 2022 figuring it all out.

I wasn't quite an old hand at this yet, but I knew how the mechanics of it worked now. If this is how I was going out of this world, then I was going to go with a bang, not a whimper.

So when I woke up on 31st December 2020, I already knew where I was going to be and what I was going to do. I had two goals in mind. Firstly I was going to get my revenge on Rob. And secondly, I was going to try and make contact with Professor Hamilton.

Revenge is a dish best served cold, so the saying goes. The position I now found myself in was a strange variation on that theme. From my perspective it had been four years ago that the bastard had screwed me over, so I'd had plenty of time to reflect on it.

But as I lie here now, next to the snoring, cheating lump beside me, I realised that for him, the dish was going to be served steaming hot – right here and now.

Get your retaliation in first might have been a more apt saying for what I had in mind.

I turned to look at him now – the man I had loved and later detested in equal measure. He was lying with his back to me, snoring away, all sixteen stone of him. He had gained at least three stone during his nine years with me.

He jokingly referred to it as contentment, but he can't have been that happy. Contented couples don't shag the neighbour unless it's in a 'car keys in the fruit bowl' kind of way. I most certainly wasn't.

His idea of contentment meant sitting around watching Sky Sports whilst simultaneously demolishing whole packets of crisps in one go. By whole packets, I don't just mean a standard bag of Walkers, I mean those big 150g bags of Doritos that you are meant to have with dips. And, yes, he used to have those, too – one of those multipack trays with four different flavours to dip in.

Usually, by the time he finished, he would have dropped crumbs all down his shirt and onto the floor. He would also have dribbled Cheese and Chive and Thousand Island dips into his ridiculous, straggly beard. It wasn't a pretty sight.

He had grown the beard purely because it was the fashion at the time and he was trying to be a hipster. He was desperate to show the younger, leaner executives coming up through his company that he was still 'with it'.

Quite what Emma next door found attractive in this slob was beyond me, but perhaps he made more of an effort for her. I had noticed in the last couple of years of our relationship that he developed a previously non-existent interest in male grooming. It wasn't all the time, just on certain days and nights. The rest of the time he was as slovenly as ever.

Looking back now, the signs that he was having an affair were obvious – after all, why would a thirty-five-year-old man spray half a can of deodorant on himself just to go and watch football down the pub? He wouldn't. He was going out with her – or round to her place. I bet he didn't treat her to the Dorito/dip beard display that I had to endure.

As I looked at the black curls of hair on the back of his head, he stirred, rolled over onto his back and loudly farted. That was enough for me; I was up and out of bed like a shot. What had I ever seen in this man?

Dressed in just my T-shirt and knickers, I headed out onto the landing and down the stairs, grabbing hold of the wooden bannister on the inside as I negotiated the triangular-shaped stairs where the staircase took a sharp hairpin bend. The stairs were very steep in this old house, probably steeper than would be allowed with modern health and safety rules and I didn't want to break my neck.

I idly wondered what would happen if I did. If I died would that be the end of it, or would I be reborn in two days? It wasn't something I had any desire to find out. That question would have to remain unanswered.

I was looking forward to reacquainting myself with my old home. It was a place that until recently I never thought I would see again. Hopefully, Rob would stay asleep long enough for me to work on the logistics of my evil plan.

What I planned to do was breathtakingly simple and that was the beauty of it. I wasn't going to do a Bobbitt and chop his dick off, or any other violent act. I was simply going to show the world what a cheating bastard he was.

It was highly possible what I was planning to do might constitute an illegal act, but I didn't care. I had heard of so-called revenge porn crimes but wasn't sure if this would fall into that category or not. It was a bit of a grey area. I wasn't going to waste time researching it; besides, even if it was a crime, it was worth it.

In the kitchen, I made myself a posh coffee using the very expensive De'Longhi coffee machine we had purchased together. Annoyingly, he had managed to keep that during what I jokingly call our 'divorce settlement', even though we weren't married.

Perversely, I wished we had been because I had come out of the relationship very badly. I never even thought while we were together about the rights or otherwise of common-law wives – something I had later cause to regret.

Health-wise I didn't feel great this morning and hadn't done since I had woken up. My throat was sore, and then I sneezed suddenly. I had all the symptoms of the early stages of a cold which triggered a memory. I did have a bad cold that New Year. If I hadn't, I would never have caught him in bed with Emma.

I took a sip of the coffee – wow, it was good and the hot liquid was soothing to my throat. I wish I had kept hold of this machine. Lily would have loved it. It made me angry just thinking about it, how much I had lost.

I thought I had got over all this, but sitting here now in the kitchen of the home I had once made my own was bringing it all back to me and it was making me angry.

Part of me was tempted to hurl the coffee machine on the floor and smash it, but what would that give me other than a brief moment's satisfaction? No, I was better than that, and besides, it could scupper my plan.

I didn't want to do anything that might jeopardise what I had in mind. If I smashed up his beloved De'Longhi he might just begin to suspect that I had rumbled him. It was OK to be angry but I needed to channel that anger effectively.

My anger melted away in an instant as I heard a telltale scratching at the kitchen door.

"Tommy!" I squealed in delight as I opened the back door to let in my beloved former pet.

After much affection and fuss which the poor cat probably didn't appreciate, coming in as he had for his breakfast, I heard the telltale creaking of the ageing floorboards from the bedroom above which told me Rob was out of bed. We lived in a 1930s semi which, despite being lovely, with large rooms and big bay windows, was also showing signs of wear and tear.

Things went quiet for a couple of minutes which meant that he would be sitting on the toilet reading yesterday's newspaper. He insisted on taking that in there with him, something that I considered to be another filthy habit. What was it with men and reading on the toilet?

Shortly afterwards, there was this horrendous noise that sounded like an aeroplane taking off which meant he had flushed the toilet. I remembered that it had been making that racket for months before I left but nothing had been done about fixing it. I had suggested a plumber but he reckoned it was just an airlock and something he could easily fix himself. He hadn't bothered, though.

A few minutes later, here he was, waltzing into the kitchen in his ill-fitting shirt, bought before he had put on weight, and tie, all set for his incredibly dull job as an accountant in the regional headquarters of a global finance company.

"Morning," I said, attempting to sound all bright and breezy in order to conceal my contempt.

"Got any coffee on?" was the grunted response. He wasn't a morning person – well, not with me anyway. I'm sure it would be different if it was Emma sitting here. Still, she probably would be soon. In my world, the one that had already happened, he hadn't wasted any time moving her in after I left. Still, it might be different this time because what I had planned for today might wreck their future. Here's hoping!

"I'll make you one," I said, turning back to the machine. As I was preparing it, I felt another sneeze coming, but rather than cover my mouth, I freely let it fly all over his coffee cup.

What's mine is yours, I thought, chuckling inwardly. What are a few germs between ex-lovers?

"Here you go," I said, turning around and handing him his coffee. He hadn't seen my act of sabotage and took it eagerly. He also hadn't bothered to say "bless you", uncaring bastard that he was.

Enjoy the cold, you bastard was what I had really wanted to say and it took a lot of restraint not to say it out loud.

"Thanks," he said. "I'd better drink this quickly – I need to get to work."

I looked at the clock above our old-fashioned electric cooker. It had one of those grills at head height that you don't see much anymore, but I liked it.

Rob didn't agree. He said it was dangerous, having melted a Tupperware box which he accidentally left on top one day when he was grilling some bacon. The resulting mess of molten plastic that dripped through had ruined his breakfast. He reckoned the kitchen was in serious need of modernisation, not that he was ever likely to fork out any money on it.

It was nearly eight-fifteen and I was eager to see the back of him, but then a wicked thought struck me. I decided I would wind him up a bit first.

"Relax," I said. "There won't be much traffic on the roads today."

Although 31st December was not a bank holiday, many people took the whole period between Christmas and New Year off. It was one of the few times of the year you could move freely around Oxford's road network without getting stuck in a jam. He had plenty of time to get to work.

"In fact," I added, emboldened by the knowledge that I had the upper hand, "we could go back upstairs for a quickie if you like?"

"Sorry, babe, I'd love to, but we've got an early meeting today," he blatantly lied. "Maybe later," he added.

I knew he would say no, that's why I had asked. I wanted to make him feel uncomfortable. We hadn't done it for months before we finished, as he always had an excuse not to. There would be no later either – he would just say he was too tired then. The truth was, he was saving himself for Emma, as his next sentence made all too obvious.

"Listen," he added, tentatively. "You are still working tonight, aren't you?"

Making sure I'm out so you can have the mistress around, no doubt?

Jeez, it was tough biting my tongue and not saying this stuff out loud.

"You know I am," I replied. "You suggested it, remember, for the extra money?"

"Yes, of course," he said. "What time are you leaving?"

"About six," I replied.

"I probably won't see you, then," he said. "We're going for a few drinks after work."

He jumped up, placed a token peck on my cheek and said, "since I won't see you later, that's to say Happy New Year."

With that, he pulled on his coat, grabbed his crappy little briefcase which he thought made him look important, and left.

"Oh, you'll see me sooner than you think," I said, out loud this time, but not until he had shut the front door behind him.

With him gone, I went to rummage around in the medicine drawer for some cold and flu remedies. I knew that this cold was going to be an absolute stinker – almost flu-like. It was so bad that I had been sent home from work with it at 2am the first time around. That had been when I had found him and Emma at it in our bed.

I wasn't going to be going to work, this time. I was going to call in sick again, but at least it would be genuine this time. That would allow me to be right here waiting to catch him out, but it wouldn't be like last time. This time, the whole world was going to see what a scoundrel he really was.

That was all to come later. Meanwhile, I had something else I wanted to do first. I returned upstairs to dress and make myself presentable, then left the house and headed into town.

I didn't live in Headington now, but just off St Clement's, closer to the city centre. I could have easily walked it, but there was a bus at the bus stop for once so I hopped on that. I was right, there was hardly any traffic on the roads and the journey only took about five minutes.

I was glad to have the shelter of the bus. It was raining, a typical dreary December drizzle and I felt bad enough with this cold as it was without getting soaked to the skin as well.

I planned to track down Professor Hamilton. I had done my homework on him and my destination was the college at which he lectured. Unfortunately, I was to be disappointed.

Other than the tourist area outside the front of the college, where tourists of various nationalities were wandering around the quadrangle, the whole college had been pretty much mothballed for the Christmas break. Most of it was locked up and when I did finally manage to find a member of staff she informed me that Professor Hamilton had gone back to Scotland for Hogmanay, as he did every year.

That was a real blow. It wasn't as if I could wait around a few weeks for term to start again. In the time frame I was trapped in he would always be away. The only other option I had was to try and track him down in Scotland and again the short time frame was going to render that difficult. I could try, but was it worth it?

The whole idea of getting help from him was a long shot anyway. This Professor might be some sort of expert in the field of time travel but that didn't mean he knew how to make it happen. All he had done had been to write a few academic papers about the theory of it.

Having me turn up in the middle of his Hogmanay celebrations like some wild-eyed lunatic claiming I was from the future was unlikely to garner a positive response unless he really did know how to time-travel and that seemed improbable.

In the end, I decided to write him a letter and address it to the college. He would get it when he got back for the new term, by which time I would be long gone, but that didn't matter. If he ever did find out how to time-travel, he ought to be able to track me down as long as I spelt out the exact details of the situation.

I walked back down Cornmarket Street, reassuringly familiar with its age-old buildings. I passed the building that had once housed HMV, a shop I had spent countless hours in during my youth. Perhaps I would get to visit it again soon, but in 2020 it had become a branch of NatWest Bank.

I turned left at the end of the street, just as Carfax Tower chimed for noon. You wouldn't have thought it was midday, so dark were the midwinter skies overhead. It was beginning to drizzle again and I was keen to get undercover. I sneezed, feeling increasingly poorly despite the three layers I was wearing.

I called into Ryman's and browsed through the writing paper pads. It was reassuring to see they had so many, even in this electronic age. Ignoring the more flowery and colourful ones, I picked up a plain white pad. I didn't want my letter to the Professor to look like some teenage girl's love letter or something in crazy, fluorescent colours from some unhinged

89

fantasist. I needed it to appear as ordinary and professional as possible.

Adding an envelope, I headed for the till where I picked up one of those BiC 4 colour pens. I had always loved them. I'd been using them since school and they were one of the few things that had stayed comfortingly the same throughout my entire life.

It was always the black or blue ink that ran out first. I rarely used red because I thought it made me look like a teacher, or green, which someone had once told me was the colour the mentally ill used. I had no idea if that were true or not but I certainly wasn't going to be writing my letter in green.

Armed with my newly acquired stationery I headed a little further along the High Street and into the Covered Market. I was making a beeline for my favourite café which had been a long-term fixture in the market. I also had fond memories of the place from when I worked there for a few months as a teenager. I was going to need these familiar points of reference as the years went by to give me stability in what was going to be a rapidly changing world.

I sat down and ordered a large breakfast and more coffee. Despite feeling poorly, I still felt hungry. What was it: feed a cold and starve a fever? That was alright, then, and I didn't have to worry about the fat content of this fry-up. Just like being able to spend whatever I wanted, food and drink were unlimited, too. The calories from this meal weren't coming back with me through time.

Whilst I was waiting for my saturated fat-laden meal to arrive, I pulled out my writing pad and started penning my letter. Pausing midway to devour my enormous brunch, I continued writing, and two cups of coffee later, my missive was ready to send:

Dear Professor Hamilton,

I am writing to you because I understand that you are a world expert in time travel and I am hoping you can help me with my unusual and possibly unique problem.

To sum it up, I have become stuck in some sort of time loop where I am spiralling back through time within my own life. Every 48 hours, at precisely 3am on 2nd January, I am cast back a year and two days in time. It first happened to me on 2nd January 2025 and has happened four more times so far. Today for me is 31st December 2020, but in another two days, it will be 31st December 2019.

I am a nurse at the John Radcliffe Hospital which is where it first happened, in a dead patient's room. There was a strange man there, waving a weird remote device about. He said his name was Doctor Gardner and he was attached to the university. He would be aged about fifty, or at least that is how old he will be in 2025. Do you know him? If you do, could you tell him about all of this? Perhaps he will know how this happened to me.

I tried to see you at the university, but you are away for the holidays, and since I am only ever here over New Year, I've no way of finding you in Oxford. By the time you come back in January, I will be gone, or at least this version of me will be. Maybe there's another version of me still here – if so, maybe you could find her?

Or if there is any way at all you can help me, can you come and find me on a New Year's Eve either now or in the future? I am enclosing a list of all the addresses I have ever lived at and when I lived at each one. Here's hoping.

Yours sincerely,

Amy Reynolds.

All I could do now was post the letter and hope for something to happen. Did I expect that anything would? It seemed unlikely. Even if he did believe me, the chances of this Professor Hamilton knowing how to travel through time seemed slim.

The same couldn't be said of my waistline after my mammoth breakfast, but it would save me from having to worry about eating for the rest of the day. I was going on a stake-out tonight and I could be holed up for some time.

I hauled myself up out of the chair and headed for the postbox on Carfax. With the letter duly despatched, that concluded the first half of my business for the day. The second half was going to be all enjoying myself. If all went to plan, I was going to get a lot of pleasure from the wanton act of revenge I had planned.

Chapter Eight
2021

I heard Big Ben chiming on the TV downstairs, the pop of a champagne cork, and Rob and Emma's laughter.

In contrast to the good time they were having, I was in abject discomfort, hidden inside the walk-in wardrobe in my bedroom. I had been there now for several hours and I was desperate for the loo but I couldn't leave now – not if I didn't want to risk messing things up.

They were still laughing and chinking glasses downstairs. How much longer were they going to be? I had assumed that if they were having an affair they'd be straight into bed as soon as I was out of the way, but that hadn't been the case. Unless they had been at it on the sofa, but I hadn't heard anything. I certainly hadn't anticipated being holed up here the entire evening.

My cold wasn't helping either. I felt lousy and my nose was dripping and I hadn't brought any tissues in with me. Fortunately, I just happened to be next to one of Rob's expensive Italian suits, so I was able to put the sleeves to good use.

It was no good – I was going to have to go but I couldn't leave the wardrobe. Even at my relatively light weight compared to Rob, I would make the decaying floorboards creak. I would just have to find something to use in the wardrobe.

Using my phone as a torch, I scanned the floor until my eyes alighted on his golf shoes. They would do very nicely. As long as I positioned myself carefully, I ought to be able to fill one of them up without them overflowing.

Hopefully, they wouldn't leak either. I was pretty sure he had told me they were waterproof. He hadn't said anything about them being piss-proof, but then the manufacturers probably hadn't envisaged this scenario in their prelaunch testing.

Relief flooded through me as urine flooded out of me into one of the ridiculously bright green shoes. Why did golfers wear such ludicrous outfits? Job done, I carefully placed the shoe at the back of the wardrobe. I didn't want to stick my foot in it later. I'd leave that particular delight for him to enjoy at a later date.

I got myself back into my previous position, hoping I would not have to wait too much longer. Settling into place, directly behind the two-inch gap I had left in the sliding doors, I picked up the weapon with which I was going to wreak my revenge. Not a gun, a knife, or a cleaver, just a simple seven-inch Android tablet.

I may have relieved my bladder, but now I had another problem to contend with, namely a nosy cat, who was scratching at the wardrobe door, curious to know why his owner had taken to hiding in cupboards.

"Go away, Tommy," I hissed. I had been delighted to reacquaint myself with my old pet this morning, but now he was threatening to let my proverbial cat out of the bag.

I opened the door just enough to shoo him away, then I had to get myself back into position quickly as I could finally hear footsteps on the stairs. The door burst open, and Emma led Rob playfully by the hand into the bedroom. She certainly seemed to know her way around the place alright – she had clearly been up here before. I felt disgusted, wondering how many times her head had been on my pillow.

The cat looked disgusted, too, and he slunk out of the room.

Thanks, Tommy, at least someone around here's got some loyalty.

Holding the tablet steady, I pressed the button which was to start broadcasting the live action.

Oh yes, this wasn't just some video I was going to humiliate or blackmail him with later. This was making full use of social media to broadcast the video of his infidelity live to the watching world.

If I had set this up correctly, Rob's friends and family should be getting a notification about now along the lines of "Rob West is live now". They would then be able to see the action unfold right in front of them. Hopefully, it wasn't too late and they had all gone to bed. On a normal night, they most probably would have, but fortunately, this was New Year.

My plan wasn't foolproof. Several things could have gone wrong. Rob might have spotted the gap in the wardrobe door and closed it. His tablet might not have been logged into Facebook, ready for this ultimate frape. The two of them might not have left the light on, turning my video into an audio-only broadcast. Better than nothing, but not as easily identifiable as him, even if it was coming from his account.

Thankfully, none of those things happened. He was about to broadcast to the world what an absolute shit he really was.

The two of them were locked in a passionate kiss, hands ripping at each other's clothes. Then Emma pulled away briefly, and with a lustful look in her eyes said, "Are you sure Amy's not going to be back tonight?"

"No chance," he replied. "The stupid cow won't be back for hours."

Oh, you've done it now, I thought.

Far from hurting me, being long past caring, his words filled me with glee. He had painted an even worse picture of himself than I could have hoped for. The reaction he was going to get for that ought to be enough alone to condemn him.

If I was lucky this whole thing might go viral and the whole world would end up despising him, never mind his friends and family.

The two of them practically fell onto the bed, and I carried on filming as the clothes came off. Within five minutes, she had her back to me, long, red, curly locks bouncing around down her back as she rode him.

It felt rather odd watching other people having sex in this way. I had never seen myself as voyeuristic or had any interest in taking part in dogging or any other such dubious activities, but I was getting a great deal of pleasure out of this. It wasn't sexual pleasure, but the satisfaction that I was getting from carrying out a successful act of revenge.

Did that make me a bad person? Whatever, I didn't care.

Holding the tablet as steady as I could in my hand, I could see the comments starting to come in below the video which simply enhanced my pleasure even more.

WTF Rob – how could you do that to Amy?

That was one of the more polite ones, from a mutual female friend.

You wanker, I'm going to chop your bollocks off and shove them down your throat.

That was a less restrained offering from his mate Gary, a dead fit and rock-hard rugby player, who I knew had always had a soft spot for me. I certainly wouldn't mind him offering me a shoulder to cry on.

But topping the lot and my undisputed favourite came from his dad and simply read:

You've brought shame upon this family, boy.

There were many, many more. It turned out my timing had been spot on, as there were many people on social media wishing each other a Happy New Year. I doubt any of them had expected to see anything like this.

The video was bound to get reported and taken down shortly, but no matter – the damage was done. And now it was about time to put the icing on the cake. I couldn't see Rob, but judging by the noise he was making, he wasn't far off from deploying his troops. It was time to make my presence known.

I shoved the wardrobe door aside as hard as I could so it made a loud bang as it hit the side, triumphantly stepped into the room, and uttered as loudly as I could, "Surprise!"

It certainly was for them. Emma leapt off him, job not quite finished with a cry of "What the fuck?!"

With her out of the way, I had a clear view of his face which had a look of pure horror on it.

"Busted!" I declared, triumphantly, still pointing the tablet right at him. As I did so, I heard his phone beeping in the pocket of his jeans which he had discarded by the side of the bed a few minutes previously.

"Oh, you might want to get that," I added. "I think your dad might be trying to get hold of you."

I was relishing all of this as I watched him squirm, still holding the tablet in front of me.

"Are you…are you filming this?" he stammered as the full horror of the situation began to sink in.

"Yep, you're live on TV right now," I said, grinning. "Jools is going to have to come up with something pretty special for his Hootenanny next year to top this!"

Emma was hurriedly putting her clothes on, panicking as she tried to put a sock on and losing her footing, causing her to fall back onto the bed. I turned the camera back towards her and she made a lame attempt to cover her face.

"Don't point that at me," she hissed. "What the hell are you doing here anyway? – he said you were at work."

"Oh, I'm sorry," I said in a blatantly insincere tone. "I just live here. Ladies and gentlemen, if you're still watching this is Emma Richards, of Jeune Street in Oxford. Now remind us, Emma, what is it you do again? Ah yes, that's right: you're a primary school teacher, aren't you? Well, what an example to set to the younger generation this is, I must say."

"Turn that fucking thing off!" she screamed and tried to grab the tablet from me, but I neatly sidestepped her.

"Tut-tut, I hope you don't use language like that in the classroom. It's hardly Topsy and Tim, is it?"

I was absolutely loving this.

She lashed out again, this time successfully knocking the tablet out of my hands and sending it flying across the room. It hit the wall and landed face-down. It had probably smashed the screen, but that didn't matter now. The damage had been well and truly done.

"Ah, that wasn't very sporting, Emma, was it?" I teased. "Rob's friends were enjoying that. Never mind, you can watch it back on the internet later, assuming it hasn't been deleted. You never know, someone might load it up onto SpankWire. You'll be famous."

"You complete bitch!" she screamed. She had totally lost it.

"Yes, I rather think I am," I added. "Now I think you had better get dressed and skedaddle. You can't go outside in just your underwear and one sock, can you? It's mighty chilly out there tonight, I should imagine. It usually is at this time of year – and I should know."

"Amy...I'm sorry," said Rob from the bed, looking all pathetic and mournful. Well, if he thought that was going to work he was sorely mistaken. It hadn't worked the first time around when I still cared, so it certainly wouldn't now.

"And you can take this sorry specimen with you," I added. "You're welcome to him."

He was too weak and shocked to argue, and within five minutes I was ushering the pair of them out of the door. Mission accomplished.

Now that it was all over, I went to the kitchen and poured myself a large glass of champagne from the half-drunk bottle left over from their earlier celebrations. It had gone a little flat by now, but certainly not as flat as their evening.

Champagne in hand, I went through to the living room and put a couple of logs on the fire. It was a feature many of the houses in this area still had and I loved it.

As I sat sipping on their champagne, I reflected on a job well done. All things considered, it had been a fine evening's work. Once I had finished, I started on an unopened bottle of Bacardi left over from Christmas and sat watching the flames flickering in front of me until tiredness claimed me.

When I awoke, I was still on the sofa. Daylight was pouring into the room now and the fire was down to a few embers. I flicked the TV on, which was showing some kids' panto. I had a raging hangover.

I had celebrated rather too well and the streaming cold I still had was making things worse. Perhaps if I was planning to drink this much again I should do it on the second night of each of my trips so I could escape the hangover when I jumped back in time. Never mind, it had definitely been worth it. Now it was time to see what additional fallout there had been from the previous night's work.

I checked my phone to find that the offending video had been deleted. That was no surprise. I don't know if he had deleted it himself or if it had been censored, but it didn't matter. The damage had been done.

I also noticed that quite a few people had posted on my wall. Many of these were simple birthday wishes from people who hadn't seen the video, but judging by the numbers asking if I was OK, many had. I also had a stack of private messages expressing varying degrees of sympathy towards me and anger towards Rob.

I replied to each one, playing the hapless victim to the hilt. So what if I had engineered the situation to cause him the maximum damage? He was still the one who had committed the crime.

One message, in particular, stood out. It was from Gary, his rugby-playing friend.

He's a tosser, and you'll be better off without him. I'm gonna kill him when I get hold of him, don't you worry. I'm really sorry you've had to go through this, Amy. If there's anything I can do, please let me know.

Oh, there was plenty Gary could do for me – or should I say to me. He was hot and I knew full well he fancied the arse off me. It had only been a matter of chance that I hadn't ended up with him in the first place. Had things happened differently the night we first met, I may well have ended up with him, rather than Rob.

Nothing had ever happened between the two of us because, unlike Rob, I was the faithful type and Gary wasn't the type to mess about with a mate's girlfriend. Maybe I could find some way to change that. Why not? I had already decided I was going to live life to the full and here was a prime example of a missed opportunity I could have a second crack at.

I thought back to the night when I had first met Rob and Gary. Back then, when I was still in my mid-twenties, my main drinking buddy and partner in crime had been Kelly, a girl I had been at school with.

We were out on the town every Friday and Saturday night without fail, revelling in our youth. Back then it seemed that those carefree times would never end, but eventually, life moved on and we went our separate ways. Nothing lasts forever.

It had been on my birthday, back in 2012, when Kelly and I had met Rob and Gary for the first time. We had been in a pub down George Street when they had started chatting us up at the bar. We accepted their offer of a drink and an invitation to sit with them followed.

Those first few minutes were crucial in deciding the outcome of not only the evening but also the next nine years. There's an unwritten rule in the dating game that when two men and two women meet on a night out, it is decided very quickly who is going to go with whom. Whether that happens verbally or through body language, once the lines of battle have been established you don't cross them.

Both Kelly and I were drawn to Gary initially, but she was more forceful in the short walk to the table, getting there ahead of me and plonking herself down next to him. It was a small, circular, bench-style sofa that surrounded a small table in a booth with room for just four.

Kelly had engineered things successfully by sitting in such a way that left me with no option but to go round to the other end of the sofa and squeeze in next to Rob. Thus, we were seated clockwise in a semicircle with Kelly on one end, then Gary, then Rob, and then me.

The boundaries were well and truly laid down and now had to be adhered to. Kelly had well and truly staked her claim to

Gary, so I was left with Rob. Something as simple as who sat where at a table in a pub was enough to change my destiny. If we stop and look back we can probably all see that our lives have been full of these seemingly inauspicious forks in the road that have life-changing consequences.

She shagged Gary that very night and had a brief and passionate fling with him that soon fizzled out. By the time it did, I was going out with Rob.

I hadn't thought about it much since then, but Gary's message had left me thinking about what might have been. Now maybe it could be. With that first meeting taking place at New Year, it seemed I was going to be given a second shot at it.

Things changed between Kelly and me soon after that when she met Mr Right. She quickly settled down, and within two years had got married. I was head bridesmaid but after that, our friendship declined. Our nights out dwindled until she got pregnant, which spelt the beginning of the end of our friendship.

We still liked each other's stuff on Facebook and wished each other Happy Birthday for a while, but even that dwindled after a while. We were in two different camps now – the parents and the non-parents. Judging by the constant stream of pictures of her with other mothers and babies on her timeline, she only had time for those in the former camp now.

Then a few years later I noticed she had unfriended me. It took me ages to work out why, but in the end, I figured it must have been because of a comment I wrote on a local Facebook group.

Someone had been complaining about some local primary school kids who had been plastering rude graffiti all over the local bus stops. When some do-gooder suggested it might not be their fault because they might have ADHD, I had written underneath:

ADHD? Isn't that just a posh modern term for what our parents used to call being a little shit?

In hindsight, it wasn't the most sensible thing to write, not with all the snowflakes around who get so easily offended these days. It was meant as a joke and, although I got a lot of Likes, some people didn't see the funny side. I got slated in a lot of the comments underneath.

It was around this time that Kelly unfriended me. I didn't make the connection at first but later I remembered. She had a lot of problems with her eldest son who had ADHD.

I missed her and the times we had shared. Soon I would get to live some of them again, including that fateful night with Gary and Rob. I didn't feel a huge amount of loyalty towards her, bearing in mind how she had dropped me after getting married. Her thing with Gary hadn't gone anywhere in the long term anyway, so I would make sure she wouldn't muscle her way to the table in front of me this time.

As for Gary, well he fell squarely into the category of unfinished business. Already I was making plans for him – and they did not just involve the night of that first meeting.

I had derived a huge amount of pleasure out of humiliating Rob in the way I had, but why stop there? I was on a roll and wanted to play up my winnings.

The phrase, 'get your retaliation in first', popped into my head. I already had done it to great effect with the video, but there was no reason why I couldn't go in for a second helping.

I made my way downstairs, desperate for some coffee to relieve my parched tongue and throat. Already the seeds of a new devious plan were beginning to form in my mind. Inwardly, I was chuckling uncontrollably, like some evil madman in an old B movie as I once again plotted and schemed.

Those B-movie villains and I had one thing in common and that was power. I could use mine for good or I could use it for evil. What I was doing was possibly a bit of both, but whichever it was, I could see how easily one could be consumed by the desire for revenge, especially if one had the means to do it.

Those baddies in those old films often had some sort of superpower and I certainly had mine. Using it for making mischief was becoming quite addictive.

I needed to tell myself that I wasn't a baddie. I wasn't planning to take over the world or unleash a global apocalypse. I was just stitching up an unfaithful boyfriend and if this was a movie, I am pretty sure that women the world over would be cheering me on.

I could get Gary to come round right now but perhaps it was worth waiting. If I played this right I could cause even more pain and humiliation for Rob than I already had. Plus, with the hangover and the cold I wasn't feeling particularly sexy. I would wait until my next jump back. That would give me ample time to plot my next diabolical plan.

As far as the rest of the day went, I was at somewhat of a loose end. I felt lousy and just wanted to go back to bed, but I didn't have the luxury of days to squander in that way. I'd never been much of a subscriber to the "seize the day" mentality, but in my current situation that was exactly what I needed to do.

My mind was made up. I definitely wasn't sitting around the house all day. Besides, Rob might try and get back in and I really couldn't be dealing with that. I'd had my fun and had no desire to get bogged down in a post-mortem.

Credit card in hand, I got back on the phone and found myself the swankiest hotel I could in London. This turned out to be remarkably easy and much cheaper than I expected. I guess they didn't have a huge number of bookings on New Year's Day. The previous night would have been a different matter, but many of those who had stayed over for the fireworks would be going home today.

I dosed myself up with Lemsip, booked a taxi to take me to the station, and within an hour of arriving at Oxford station found myself in Central London.

I went for a walk around Harrods looking at all the things I could buy if I so desired, but there seemed little point as I couldn't take any of it back through time with me. In the end, I just settled on a very expensive silk negligee that no one else would ever see but I could wear tonight to make me feel good.

Then I took myself off to my £800-a-night hotel where I got a pleasant surprise when the man on the desk offered me a free upgrade to the penthouse suite. I gave them my credit card details and told them to charge everything to that. Then I got on with the business of spoiling myself rotten – massages, spa, room service, the lot.

I was all alone but I didn't care. This was pure self-indulgence and I was going to squeeze as much out of the experience as I could. I was getting such a buzz out of it that my hangover soon disappeared and even my cold seemed to abate. It was amazing what a little pampering could do for the body and soul.

As the day wound down, and I glugged down £150 bottles of wine, in my little silk negligee in my penthouse suite, I formulated the next stage of my plan for the next day. By the time I had finished, I was quite drunk again – both on the wine and the power – but at least there would be no hangover to worry about this time.

If everything went to plan, Rob was in for another bad day.

Chapter Nine
2019

I was woken by the pulsing of the alarm from the speaker next to my bed.

"Alexa, stop," I said, keen to shut her up before she woke Rob. She obeyed and the sound ceased, leaving him thankfully still snoring in bed beside me. He was in exactly the same position as he had been before and the room smelled, suggesting he had been letting off in his sleep again.

I felt a sense of déjà vu – something I guess I was going to be experiencing a lot.

Being woken up by Alexa while it was still dark at this time of year meant I must be on a day shift at work. I had forgotten to check my diary to find out, but it didn't matter. I wasn't going in anyway.

Taking care not to wake him, I took my bag into the bathroom, turned on the light and checked my diary. I was indeed due in for 8am. I also noted that it was a Tuesday, which meant there was a good chance he would be working, too. I was counting on him being out of the house today as an essential part of my latest dastardly scheme, which I now went over once again as I performed my morning ablutions.

My initial desire for revenge had been temporarily sated by my bit of fun with the video, but now I thirsted for more. I wanted him to feel the pain and the humiliation of discovering your partner in bed with someone else.

Was I being overly vindictive? Maybe, but he had really hurt me at the time and it seemed only fair he should get a taste of his own medicine.

I had another eight years to play with and had wondered whether doing what I planned to do in this particular year was the best timing. It was only a year before we had broken up and I later found out he had been sleeping with Emma for at least three years before that. So that meant the affair was going on now.

If I did the dirty on him this year, would he even be that bothered? My plan could backfire. What if he cared for me so little by this time that my betrayal might be an opportunity for him? It could be the green light he had been waiting for to get rid of me and legitimise his relationship with Emma.

If I waited a few more years until before Emma had come along, would that be more effective? And would it be fair? I genuinely believe we were happy back then, so I could hurt him a lot more, but was it morally right to do that? Would I be punishing an innocent man for crimes he had yet to commit?

I decided I didn't want to wait. I had my mind set on a particular course of action and I didn't want to waste any time. There were other reasons, too. Gary, my intended conquest, was single right now and would probably be highly receptive to my advances if I approached him in the right way.

Further back in time, he would be in a relationship, and I didn't want to mess that up for him unnecessarily before it came to its natural end. Plus, there's no guarantee that he would even consider sleeping with me when he had a girlfriend. From what I had seen he didn't mess around when he was in a relationship, unlike some I could mention.

I wasn't even sure if I was going to be able to persuade him that sleeping with his best mate's girl was a good idea. I was going to have to come up with something pretty convincing, I knew that. His reaction to Rob's cheating in the video was the key to all this. I just needed to provoke that reaction and the rest should fall into place.

By the time I was showered, dressed and ready to go, Rob was stirring. I went downstairs, and made him a cup of coffee, wishing I could lace it with something. Unfortunately, we were right out of polonium-210 so I settled for two sugars, took it up and plonked it down on the bedside table.

"You are working today, aren't you?" I inquired. I got a perverse satisfaction out of asking this question because it was exactly what he had asked me when planning his New Year love-fest with Emma.

"Yes, babe," he said.

Don't babe me, you tosser.

That was what every fibre of my being wanted to scream out in response but I managed to restrain myself.

"See you tonight, then," I replied instead with exaggerated cheerfulness, as I flounced out of the room, not wanting to prolong the conversation any longer than was necessary.

I knew all I needed to know. He was working so would be home no later than 6pm, possibly earlier if his office clocked off a bit early for New Year.

I hadn't bothered to check what we were supposed to be doing tonight and couldn't remember. I was five years in my past now and my memories of the time had faded.

Not that it mattered as any plans for tonight would be blown out of the water by what I had lined up. Still, I ought to have been more prepared so I made a mental note to try and find out these things in advance from now on. I needed to be better prepared.

Right now, I just needed to concentrate on today's act of revenge. I felt a real buzz of excitement at the thought of what I was about to do. Not only was I going to take him down all over again, but as a bonus, I was going to get a bloody good shag out of it, too.

There's part of me that can hardly believe I'm even thinking or planning these things. I've always been one of the good girls – never getting detentions at school or anything like that. My current behaviour is quite out of character for me.

Is it because I've been let off the leash and there are no longer any consequences? What would happen if we found out the world would end in a month? Would everyone cast off their inhibitions and throw caution to the wind the way I currently was?

I couldn't deny it was extremely exhilarating. My impending demise had made me feel more alive and full of purpose than I ever had. I had heard the acronym YOLO (you only live once) being used a lot by younger people in recent years to justify risky behaviour.

In my case, it was more like you only live twice which could have been a great title if my story ever got made into a film. Unfortunately, James Bond got there first.

In my current frame of mind, I was hell-bent on squeezing out every last drop of whatever time I had left on this planet. Whether that was revenge, sexual fantasies or any other hedonistic pleasures, I wasn't going to waste a single opportunity.

I left the house, pretending to go to work, but, as was becoming the norm, I had absolutely no intention of going. It was great, this – I could skive off work as often as I wanted and I never got into trouble for it. I didn't even need to bother phoning in sick if I didn't want to, but I thought it best to, anyway. Even if there were no long-term consequences, I didn't want the hospital pestering me all day trying to find out where I was.

It was absolutely freezing outside. There had been a hard frost overnight and the grass verge alongside the pavement had a thick, white crust on it where the sun hadn't got to it yet.

Why had my time loop had to happen in the middle of winter? Would I ever feel the warmth of the sun on my skin again? Then I remembered the Christmas and New Year I had spent in Australia. At least I still had that to look forward to.

I rang the hospital as I walked down the street, hanging up just as I turned right into St Clement's. I stopped off at the nearest café to grab some breakfast while I waited for Rob to bugger off to work. I made sure I sat well away from the window to avoid being spotted by him as he drove past.

Once I was sure the coast was clear, I headed back home. The houses in Jeune Street were terraced, with large bay windows. They were arranged so that each pair of houses had their front doors side by side, each house being a mirror of the one next to it.

This meant there was no hiding place when, just as I opened the gate to walk down the front path, the adjacent house's front door opened. Before I even clocked her, I knew who I was destined to see, the dreaded Emma.

"Morning, Amy," she said, all bright and breezy. "How are you, today?"

You're shagging my boyfriend, you two-faced bitch. How dare you be all sweetness and light with me!

Of course, she didn't know I knew that and I wasn't about to let on. All that business of catching her in bed with him was a year in the future. As far as she was concerned, I was just the none-the-wiser fool she was crapping all over. Well, if it was false friendliness that was the order of the day, then two could play at that game.

"Yeah, I'm all good," I said cheerily. "Got anything good planned for New Year?"

"Oh, just a quiet night in and a day at home tomorrow," she said, smiling.

111

Oh yes, a day at home tomorrow. While Rob's at home for the bank holiday and I'm working. Bitch.

"Sounds good," I replied. "Nothing too strenuous for me, either. I'm working tomorrow."

"I thought you were working today, too," she said.

And how would you know that? Does Rob give you a copy of my shift pattern so you can come round and help yourself to his body as soon as my back's turned?

"I am," I replied. "I just had to nip back home for something."

"Well, have a great New Year, Amy," she said, and walked on down the path in her ridiculously impractical heels, taking care to avoid the icy patches on the crooked paving stones on her front path.

Yeah, I hope you slip and break your neck, you slapper.

I couldn't recall a time when the words coming out of my mouth had been so far removed from what I was thinking.

"You, too, Emma – have a good one," was what I actually said. And that was that. She had lived next door for four years and the brief exchange we had just had was probably about the longest conversation we had had in all that time.

Back inside, I went straight for the coffee while I put the finishing touches to my plan. There was no point calling Gary up yet because he would be at work. He was a postman – a job that kept him very fit along with his rugby playing, I knew he normally knocked off by mid-afternoon and that would suit me perfectly.

Until then, I had a bit of time on my hands. Mindful of the mental note I had made earlier to be better prepared for my journey back through time, this seemed like an ideal time to carry out some research.

I logged on to my laptop and started to go back through my social media timeline, looking for clues, and writing down every scrap of information that might be of use to me. The actual notes would be of no use to me after this trip. I couldn't take them back through time with me, but I could read them over and over to memorise them before I went.

Finding information on the laptop was quick and easy – far easier than using a mobile phone. I couldn't understand for the life of me why laptops had fallen out of favour. By 2025, hardly anyone used them, even in the workplace. I understood the argument that phones and tablets were convenient for people on the move but even so – give me a laptop with a full-size screen and a proper keyboard any day. I could just get so much more done.

I had fond memories of this trusty old ASUS laptop. It had served me well for many years. I bought it back in around 2012 and here it was, in 2019, still going strong.

I went back through Facebook as far as I could. The trail stopped at New Year's Eve 2007, which was the year I had joined. What I did find gave me a pretty good snapshot of the years 2007-2018, enough to ascertain roughly where I had been each year.

None of it was particularly exciting and made me think perhaps I had wasted the best years of my life. I could and should have been doing so much more. I would have to see what I could do to change that second time around.

What about prior to 2007? I had been 21 then. How was I going to find out more about my teenage years? Email was no good – that didn't go back past 2012 on this computer. I had used email long before that, but it seems that when I got this laptop, I didn't bring any archive material with me, or if I did, I had no idea where I had stored it.

Where else could I look for clues? There might be something upstairs that could help. I went up, rummaged around in the bottom of my wardrobe and pulled out an old, tartan, shortbread tin. It was the box I'd kept my teenage memories in and I hadn't opened it for years.

I prised open the lid, revealing a stash of keepsakes. My eyes were instantly drawn to the letters from my first love, Max. Oh, how I had loved him when we were sixteen. He was so sweet on me, and so old-fashioned, sending me handwritten declarations of love on what was now faded yellow paper. He also had beautiful italic handwriting, written with a proper fountain pen, something you hardly ever see these days.

You hardly even saw it then. Love letters on real paper had been a dying art form even in 2002. By then, SMS texting had become ubiquitous for my generation.

I picked up a few of the letters and read through them, feeling full of nostalgia for those innocent times. Maybe I should have made more effort to hold onto Max. It had seemed at sixteen that we would be inseparable forever but we grew up and he had gone away to university in Manchester.

He wasn't far away from my own roots in Liverpool, but I was well and truly established in Oxford by then. With my dad dying when I was only fifteen, and his parents gone, I no longer had any family links back home on Merseyside.

I delved deeper into the box. There were a few old concert tickets, one of which caught my eye right away. It was for Kylie Minogue's Showgirl tour which I had gone to see at Wembley Arena. The date on the ticket read 31st December 2006. It seemed I was destined to see Kylie again.

Fond memories were replaced by sad ones as I pulled out a postcard from Thailand, sent by my sister, Rachel, on the 15th of December 2004. It hadn't arrived until mid-January the following year and was the last time I or anyone else had ever heard from her. She had been missing, presumed dead, for several weeks by then.

I shed more than a few tears as I read the card. At the turn of the millennium, I had a father, sister and mother. Barely a decade into the new century, they were all dead and I was an orphan at twenty-five.

I had never given up hope that one day Rachel might return, but I knew that it was highly unlikely. She had almost certainly perished, swept into the sea like so many thousands of others, on that devastating morning of Boxing Day, 2004.

It was time to put my memories away for now. The rumbling in my stomach told me it was well past lunchtime. Placing the lid back on the tin, I headed downstairs to make myself something to eat.

As I munched on a cheese and pickle sandwich, I read the notes I had made over and over again. It wasn't a complete snapshot of my life by any means, but enough to give me a broad outline of what to expect in the weeks ahead.

With lunch out of the way, it was time to call Gary. He would be finishing work soon if he hadn't already. I didn't imagine there would be that much post to deliver at this time of year. The big rush would have been all before Christmas.

Preparing myself for the dramatic piece of acting I was about to try and pull off, I picked up my mobile, which had now reverted to an S9, browsed through my contacts until I found Gary's number, and pressed.

He answered really quickly, within one ring. He was certainly on the ball today.

"Hey, gorgeous – how's it going?" he asked. That was a promising start.

I'd had good practice at putting on my sickly voice for phoning into work the past few days. Now it was time to play the damsel in distress. Putting on the most miserable-sounding voice I could muster without actually sobbing, I got straight to the point.

"Oh, Gary, it's not going well at all," I replied. "It's Rob. You know that girl Emma that lives next door? Well, I've just found out he's been cheating on me with her."

"The bastard!" exclaimed Gary. "I knew he was up to something. That's why he hasn't come down the pub for months."

"Well, that's news to me," I replied, adding, "He goes out every Sunday, supposedly to do the quiz with you in Port Mahon."

"First I've heard of it. What an arsehole. I'm so sorry, Amy. Is there anything I can do?"

"Could you come round?" I said, actually managing to produce quite a convincing sob. "I'm feeling really upset."

"I'm on my way," he said. "I'll be there in five. I'm only just up the road."

After he rang off, I started to have doubts about what I was planning to do. I had no qualms about making Rob's life a misery, but Gary was a decent chap and I wasn't sure dragging him into all of this was entirely fair.

Still, he fancied the arse off me and would be up me like a rat up a drainpipe under the right circumstances. And that was today. Yes, maybe I was just using him to get back at Rob but it's not like he wasn't going to get some benefit from it.

Rob, of course, had no idea that I knew about him and Emma. He was going to be in for a shock.

Casting aside my doubts, I needed to put the finishing touches to my upset persona. I only had a couple of minutes, so I grabbed an onion from the fridge and took it over to the kitchen surface next to the sink. I grabbed a chopping board and knife from the drainer and got to work. Quickly I chopped the onion up and then stuck my face right down by the chopping board to breathe in the fumes.

It stung like hell, but had the desired effect – my eyes were running like waterfalls. Right on cue, the doorbell rang. Grabbing the board, I swept the chopped onions out of sight into the kitchen bin, placed it back on the side and made my way to the hall.

Before answering the door I made a brief diversion into the cloakroom to rinse my hands and check my look in the mirror. Big, puffy red eyes looked back at me. Perfect.

Opening the door, I was pleased to see Gary looking as buff as ever, in his postman's uniform. Despite the freezing weather, he was still wearing shorts – what was it about postmen and shorts in all weathers? I really ought to ask him, but I had other things on my mind right now.

"Oh Gary, thank you so much for coming," I blurted out in as dramatic a voice as I dared. "I can't believe this is happening to me."

As soon as he was in the flat, I flung my arms around him and said, "Please, just hold me," adding a few sobs in for good measure.

"I'm so sorry Rob's done this to you, Amy," said Gary, his face out of view over my shoulder. "You deserve better."

I pulled away so I could face him, but made sure he didn't let go. With his arms still around me and looking at my most needy, I replied. "I do."

When I leaned in for the kiss, he didn't reject me. Ten minutes later, we were in bed.

What had I been missing all these years? Sex with him was amazing. It wasn't just that he was fitter or that he was bigger where it mattered – which he was, by a considerable margin. He was just considerate, putting my needs first.

Not for the first time I cursed that night in the bar back in 2012 when Kelly had got in first. All of this could have been mine, legitimately, without the need to resort to all this subterfuge.

As we lay in the afterglow, daylight fading outside through the still-open curtains, I glanced across at the clock on the bedside table. It was a little after 4pm. Rob probably wouldn't be home for a couple of hours yet so I needed to keep Gary here. I wanted Rob to find us in bed together, just as I'd found him and Emma.

As if he'd read my mind, Gary asked, "Where is Rob, now?"

"He's gone," I lied. "When I found out, he moved in next door with her temporarily. He said I needed to be out of this place by the end of this week, and then he and Emma were moving back in. She's only renting a room next door."

There was no reason that Gary should disbelieve this. Rob's toiletries and things were still all around the room, but since I had said he had only gone temporarily, that wouldn't seem out of place.

"That's good," said Gary. "I wouldn't want him finding us in bed together, even if he has been at it with Emma."

I felt a pang of guilt about dragging Gary into this. Was I doing the right thing? It was too late to back down now. I had come this far, I had to see it through.

"It would be no more than he'd deserve," I said.

"Is that how you found out?" asked Gary. "Were they at it in here?"

"Nothing so dramatic," I said. "I was suspicious because he was always fiddling around on his phone and always locked it

118

before he put it down. Sooner or later I knew he would slip, and, sure enough, he did on Christmas Day when he'd had so much wine at lunchtime he fell asleep in front of The Queen."

"So you took the opportunity to look at his phone?" asked Gary.

"Yes," I replied. "They had been sending dirty messages to each other on Messenger, including pictures, as well as making plans to meet up. When I confronted him with it a couple of days ago he confessed everything."

"Well, if you need somewhere to stay, I've got a spare room," he offered.

"I may just take you up on that," I replied.

I had fabricated the vast majority of this story but the details didn't matter. The basic fact that Rob was sleeping with Emma still stood, no matter how I had found out. And so far it had all been so worth it. Gary had just satisfied me more than anyone had for as long as I could remember, and now I wanted more.

When 6pm rolled around, we were at it hard for a third time. Three times in one afternoon! That was going some. I couldn't remember the last time Rob had managed it three times in a calendar month, not with me anyway. I'm sure Emma next door was getting plenty, though.

Despite being in the rapturous throes of yet another climax, I was fully aware of the time and kept half an ear open. When I heard the telltale sound of Rob's key in the lock, I seriously upped the decibels so that Gary wouldn't hear him. I'm talking serious porn-star levels of moaning here.

I'd like to claim it as another string to my recently acquired acting bow but quite honestly, there wasn't a huge amount of acting required, not with the effect Gary was having on me.

It worked anyway because Gary didn't hear Rob but Rob certainly heard us. Just as my moaning pushed Gary over the edge, the bedroom door was flung open.

"What the fuck!" exclaimed Rob.

Ironically, that is exactly what it was. It must have been one of the very few occasions when that phrase was actually uttered in the correct context. It was also the exact same line I had used the first time I had caught him at it with Emma, but the boot was on the other foot this time.

"I don't believe this!" shouted Rob. "My girlfriend and my best mate."

Gary leapt up, ready to defend himself in case Rob tried anything. "You can't talk, mate – she's told me all about you and that Emma next door."

"What's sauce for the goose," I chipped in, eager to fan the flames. I was interested to see where this was going to go.

"What are you talking about?" said Rob.

He was clearly going to try and deny it, but he wasn't as good at acting as I was. The brief flash of recognition that had crossed his face when Gary had mentioned Emma had already betrayed him and he knew it. Rob was like an open book. It was a good job he didn't play poker because he would be giving off tells left, right and centre.

"She's told me all about it, mate," replied Gary, quickly pulling on his boxers, and reaching for his shorts.

Good move, I thought. Being naked in a confrontation is never an advantage.

"Well even if I was, that's not as bad as this," Rob claimed.

"How do you figure that?" I asked, keen to hear how he was going to try and justify himself.

"It's completely different," argued Rob. "You hardly know Emma but he's my best mate. That's a much worse betrayal."

"You arsehole," said Gary, and thumped him square in the jaw with a clean right hook. Rob sprawled backwards in surprise onto the bed. Gary turned away and pulled on his shirt.

For the first time I started to worry that this could potentially start getting out of hand, "That's enough," I said. With Gary now fully dressed, I shepherded him out of the room, just as Rob was getting to his feet, blood trickling from a cut on his lower lip.

"You haven't heard the last of this!" shouted Rob furiously.

I hadn't expected him to be this angry, bearing in mind what he and Emma had been doing. Perhaps it was more down to being humiliated by his mate than my infidelity. Being thumped probably hadn't helped either. I hadn't expected Gary to do that. Things had gone far enough.

"You'd better go," I said, ushering Gary quickly down the stairs and into the kitchen where he had taken off his shoes. But it wasn't over yet. Rob was hot on our heels. This wasn't funny and the situation was about to escalate rapidly.

"Oh no, you don't get away that easily!" he screamed hysterically, bursting into the kitchen as Gary was putting on his shoes. The blood was congealing in his beard now.

"For fuck's sake, mate, do you want some more?" said Gary aggressively. "You know I could have you, anytime."

He was right. Rob was puny in comparison – his five-foot-nine paunchy frame was a complete mismatch against six-foot muscle-man Gary, but Rob's blood was up and he wasn't thinking straight. He lunged forward, making an amateurish swing at Gary which the stronger man easily avoided.

Gary could and should have walked out then, but he couldn't resist punching Rob again. He caught him less squarely on the side of the face this time, causing Rob to reel back against the counter where I had been chopping onions earlier.

"You're a wanker and she's a slag," hissed Rob.

Gary could be quite violent when riled. I knew he had been involved in quite a few brawls in his younger days and had heard rumours of a GBH charge long before I met him. Now he advanced on his mate, anger in his eyes.

"Gary, don't!" I cried. "You've made your point, now just leave it."

As Gary went to punch Rob again, his quarry leaned back onto the counter, right hand alighting on the knife I had been using earlier. I don't think he even knew it was there until he touched it, but, desperate to defend himself, he instinctively thrust it forward and upwards, taking Gary by surprise.

Whether Rob's intention had been to make him back off, or actually stab him, I wasn't sure. The puny vegetable knife wouldn't have been enough to do serious damage in most circumstances. It was only about three inches long and not even that sharp, but on this occasion Rob got lucky – or you could say unlucky, depending on how you looked at it.

The knife didn't plunge into Gary, it caught him with more of a glancing blow, but it was where it struck that did the damage. Most places on the body would have been just a flesh wound, but this caught him right on the neck, instantly causing blood to spurt out all over the place.

"Oh my God, what have you done!?" I shouted, as Gary just stood there, motionless for a moment, a look of disbelief on his face, before slumping slowly to the floor, blood gushing out of him at an alarming rate. As a trained health professional I knew this could mean only one thing.

"You've severed an artery," I added as Rob just stood there, frozen in shock, blood draining from his face almost as fast as it was draining out of Gary's neck.

My first thought was to call an ambulance, but knew it would be too late. Rob had slashed him in such a way they wouldn't be in time. I doubted that we alone could stem the flow even if we tried. The blood was everywhere, pouring out of Gary all over the white ceramic kitchen tiles.

"What...what are we going to do?" bleated Rob pathetically. He clearly wasn't going to be any use.

There was nothing we could do. The shock of the situation had hit me just as much as it had him, but I had to stay strong. Trying to assuage feelings of guilt I told myself that this wasn't real and in two more days it would never have happened. I would safely a year in the past then and Gary would be alive and kicking.

As for the here and now Rob could deal with it. He had done it, after all.

"Don't you mean what are you going to do?" I responded. "I'm out of here."

I ran out of the kitchen, unable to bear looking at Gary's now motionless body any longer. If he wasn't dead already, he very soon would be. As I grabbed my coat and bag, desperate to be out of there, Rob called after me.

"What do you mean, you're out of here? You can't just leave me."

"I can and I will. Watch me," I replied.

"I'll say you did it," he threatened. "Your fingerprints will be on this knife."

"Whatever," I replied, pulling on my coat and heading straight for the front door. "You're on your own now. Have fun explaining it all to the police, unless your lady friend next door is willing to help you dispose of the body. Best of luck!"

And with that parting shot, I slammed the front door behind me and made good my escape.

It was only when I was safely away down the road that the full horror of what had just happened struck me.

Chapter Ten
2020

The following morning I was holed up in a room above a pub in Evesham, sick with worry and guilt. I had hardly slept all night with all the turmoil going through my mind.

How had I ended up here? My destination had been dictated by a random choice of train after I had realised I had to get out of Oxford fast.

Was I running away? Possibly and that didn't make me feel great. Everyone always said that was the coward's way out. It probably wasn't the wisest move either. Simply by fleeing the scene, I was making myself look guilty.

There was nothing to stop Rob from carrying out his threat to tell the police I did it, and who would look the more likely suspect? The man on the scene who had called the police or the woman who had fled?

Things certainly looked bad, and there was no way I would have taken this course of action if I was leading any sort of normal life. But I knew I didn't need to evade capture forever, just for a day and a half until I could escape back into the past.

It had crossed my mind that I might be storing up trouble for the theoretical other me, the one who might be left here to pick up the pieces after my mind had left this body. If she existed, what would happen to her? But then she wasn't guilty, was she? So she had nothing to worry about, right?

If I don't sound convinced, it's because I'm not. Who am I kidding? I may not have held the blade as it plunged into Gary's neck, but there was no denying I was responsible for all of this.

I had acted like a vengeful little slag, and I didn't like what I had become. I had been desperate for revenge and lustful for sex which I had acquired under false pretences. Gary hadn't asked to be dragged into my little games and had paid the ultimate price.

Why couldn't I have been satisfied with humiliating Rob with the video and left it at that? Why had I had to go in for a second bite of the cherry? Talk about abusing my powers. I was no better than those megalomaniac B-movie villains. Things needed to change and they needed to start changing right now.

With thirty-plus hours to kill, I needed to decide what to do with them. I thought about handing myself in to the police, but what would be the point? It would be best to just get out of town, run down the clock and then head back to 2018 for a fresh start.

It was unlikely anybody would be looking for me in Evesham, which was a quiet and pleasant little town across the Cotswolds from Oxford. I had only ended up here by chance and perhaps that was the best way. No clever detective would be able to follow my thought processes to deduct where I had gone, as there hadn't been any thought put into it.

After leaving the house I had first toyed with the idea of fleeing the country but quickly realised I didn't have my passport, so that was a non-starter. There was no way I was going back to get it. Booking flights would have involved using a bank card anyway which was the equivalent of putting a large flashing neon sign over my head saying "Here she is".

I couldn't afford to leave any sort of paper trail as to where I was going so I needed to deal strictly in cash from here onwards.

Stopping at the cashpoint in Headington, I took out the maximum allowed. If the police did try and track me down, that's where the trail would go cold. As soon as I had my cash, I walked to the bus stop, pausing along the way to dump my mobile phone in a bin. I wasn't having that giving away my location either.

I caught a bus into town which was packed with revellers heading out to celebrate New Year. This was one year I certainly wouldn't be celebrating.

My biggest worry now was CCTV. I had seen plenty of TV dramas where people had been tracked by it and I was in the centre of a big city, after all. My best bet was to change outfits so I headed into Debenhams, went up and down in the lift a couple of times, wandered around all over the shop and then bought a hat, scarf and new hoodie.

I took these into the toilets and changed, stuffing my old clothes into a bag to dispose of them later. Emerging from the toilets, head bowed, I hoped I had done enough to evade any attempts to track me.

Suitably disguised, I now headed straight for Oxford station, stuffing the carrier bag that now contained my old clothes into a litter bin en route. I hoped that there would still be some trains running, bearing in mind it was almost 7pm now on New Year's Eve. Thanks to it being a normal working weekday there were still a few.

Scanning the boards I decided to avoid London and the obvious big cities and instead bought a ticket for the next train departing, bound for Hereford. That sounded like a suitably anonymous sort of place to hide out for a day or two.

I sat alone on the quiet train, as far away from other people as possible. I must have had a guilty conscience because I kept imagining that everybody who walked past was looking at me accusingly, branding me a murderer with their eyes. I kept my head down, keen to hide my face, not even looking up when the guard came to clip my ticket.

127

What if they had managed to track me on CCTV all the way to Oxford station and had seen me getting on the train? Would they be waiting to arrest me at Hereford station?

I was getting a bit paranoid. I clearly wasn't thinking straight, as it was highly unlikely anyone would be looking for me so soon. Even so, I convinced myself that going to Hereford was too risky so I decided to get off the train at the next stop, which was at Evesham.

It was dark, wet and cold and all I wanted was a room for the night. With no phone, I had no way of finding out what was available, so just had to walk through the town until I found somewhere.

There was a large hotel opposite the station but I ignored that. My experience was that these sorts of places rarely took bookings in cash, and even if they did would want some sort of ID.

I needed something more anonymous like a small family B&B or a pub. I didn't rate my chances of finding either at this time of night and at this time of the year. It was hardly tourist season. But if I didn't find something soon I might face the unwelcome prospect of spending the night outside.

I ran through the options in my head. If I had been totally desperate, I could have gone to a pub, pulled some random bloke and then let him take me home for the night. But there was no way I was going to do that. In my mind, it was bordering on prostitution.

The mere fact I had even considered it as a possibility was bad enough. Had I really sunk that low – sex just to get a bed for the night? Hadn't I slagged about enough already today? What the hell was I turning into?

No, there was no way I was lowering myself to that level. I would rather freeze outside. Was it to come to that? Was I about to experience what it was like to be a homeless person in the middle of winter? Well, if I was, it was no more than I deserved, quite frankly.

I couldn't find anywhere in town that fitted my needs so I decided to just find a pub where I could at least be warm and have a drink. Even that proved problematic, as many of them had private parties on for New Year and were ticket-only.

Eventually, I found a nice old-fashioned boozer down the far end of the town with no entry restrictions. It was packed with locals enjoying a karaoke night.

Safely In the warm at last, even if it was only temporary, I got a couple of double vodkas inside me and then asked the landlord if he knew of any nearby hotels, neatly blaming why I was stranded in Evesham on a broken-down car. It was a plausible enough excuse, but it was lying, of course, something I else I frowned upon but was now being reduced to.

Fortunately, I was in luck. The pub had rooms which they occasionally let out upstairs and they agreed to let me stay the night, cash upfront, with no need for any ID. All they did was ask me my name, to which I replied with the first thing that came into my head: Helen. Another lie!

It was a great relief knowing I wouldn't have to sleep outside, not that I got a lot of sleeping done. I spent most of the night tossing and turning, racked with remorse for the events of the previous day.

Now it was the following morning, and I was still up in the room, trying to work out how to get through this last day before I moved on. Accommodation wouldn't be as big a problem tonight because I'd be jumping back in time at 3am, so I could probably stay up until that time, even if I did have to spend a couple of hours outside after the pubs shut.

I had planned to slip away from the pub quietly but my hosts insisted on giving me breakfast, which was very kind. Both they and the locals the previous evening had been very welcoming towards me. Their hospitality had got me through a difficult time and I could now face the day ahead with renewed strength.

Before I left I did have one slight problem when the landlord informed me that his brother was a mechanic who would be visiting that afternoon and would be only too pleased to take a look at my car for me. I initially tried to refuse, saying they had done more than enough for me already, but he refused to take no for an answer.

In the end, I agreed, saying I wanted to spend a little time exploring Evesham and that I would be back later. Of course, the car was nonexistent, so I had no intention of returning.

More lies, I thought. Once you started telling a few, it seemed you couldn't get out of it. One naturally led to another. That was all going to stop tomorrow. I was going to wipe the slate clean and start again.

Since I had time to kill I decided I may as well have a look around Evesham, as I had only seen it in darkness the previous evening. It was one of those rare things you get in midwinter – a sunny and relatively mild morning which was a welcome relief from the endless cold weather I was usually stuck with.

Across the road from the pub were some very pretty old medieval buildings with exposed timber beams. I walked towards stopping to read the plaques on the walls about their history. Then I walked through a churchyard and into a pretty little park which led down towards the River Avon which passed through Evesham.

Alongside the river was a lovely tree-lined avenue which reminded me of walking down to the river in Christ Church

Meadow in Oxford. The trees were bare now but I imagined they must look very pretty in full leaf during the summer.

It was quiet and calm down here which was exactly what I needed to calm my nerves and give me time to think. I sat down on a bench and watched as a couple of rowers went by, dressed in all the proper gear, clearly training for some sort of event. Maybe they had races here, like in Henley.

I knew that I had wasted my time pursuing revenge over Rob. From now on I needed to do something more constructive with my time. As I sat soaking up the weak, winter sunlight, I realised that what I longed for more than anything was to feel the heat of the sun on my face again in a warm part of the world. My life expectancy was short and I didn't want to spend it all stuck in the middle of an English winter.

I knew that there were a couple of years I would be abroad at New Year, but they were a long way off and I didn't want to wait. Tomorrow I would have 48 hours to play with. I could almost fly to the other side of the world and back in that time.

It was time to make a positive decision. Starting tomorrow, I would jet off and see the world. I had nothing else planned for the next few years, so why not?

Obviously, I couldn't book any flights or make any advance arrangements, but that could all be sorted on the day. As long as I had my passport and credit card, the world was my oyster. Well, at least the world that I could reach in a reasonable flight time was my oyster. I didn't want to spend half my life in airports or on planes.

That was the next few trips sorted, but what of today? I was at a serious loose end, with only the clothes I was dressed in and the cash I was carrying. Having left in such a hurry, I hadn't brought so much as a toothbrush with me and I was also still dressed in what I had travelled in yesterday. Although I had had a shower at the pub, I still felt like a total skank.

I walked back into town. Most of the shops were shut but I found a convenience store that was open where I bought a toothbrush, toothpaste and a can of deodorant. Then I walked back to some public toilets I had seen in the park so that I could at least attend to my basic hygiene needs.

That it should come to this – brushing my teeth in a public toilet like some sort of vagrant and on my birthday as well. This really was a low. Recriminations and regrets began to flood through my mind again. Maybe some decent food would take my mind off things. Despite the bacon and eggs I had consumed at the pub, I already felt hungry again.

I walked back to the High Street, looking for somewhere to eat that was open on New Year's Day, eventually finding a small café which was serving. There I ordered myself a plate of good old English fish and chips. This was something that always made me feel better, reminding me as it did of my childhood.

When I was a kid and we lived in Liverpool, my mum worked on Saturdays, leaving Dad to look after me and Rachel. He was under instructions to cook us something healthy for lunch but instead always took us to this wonderful chippy in West Derby. It had place mats with snakes and ladders on them which Rachel and I used to play with while we waited for our chips. I've never tasted any as good anywhere else since.

Having said that, the chips in this place were awesome, certainly the best I'd had in years. I started to relax, the comforting food helping to take the edge off my guilt and worry over recent events. But it was not to last long. Halfway through devouring my chips, along with a succulent piece of cod, I saw something that almost made me shake with fear.

I was sitting opposite a large-screen TV on the wall at the end of the café which was broadcasting rolling news from the BBC. The volume was muted but the subtitles were on. I had been idly watching the lead story which predictably was about the New Year celebrations. In my life, that was always the lead story. As I watched the usual shots of fireworks exploding outside Big Ben, they cut to a new story, including a shot of a very familiar-looking street.

It took only a split second for the realisation to kick in that this was Jeune Street. There was my house, large as life, with police tape all around it. As I read the subtitles popping up beneath I found myself almost gasping for air in shock at what I was seeing.

Police have launched a murder investigation after a man's body was discovered at a house in Oxford.

36-year-old Gary Welby was found dead when officers were called to an address on Jeune Street, at around 6.35pm on New Year's Eve. He had bled to death from a wound to the neck.

Detectives are treating the incident as murder.

A local man who has not been named was arrested at the scene but later released without bail. Police are currently seeking a woman in connection with the crime. 34-year-old Amy Reynolds, who it is believed lived at the address, has not been seen since the crime.

As the last sentence was read out, a picture of me appeared on the screen. I recognised it straight away – it was my profile picture from Facebook and had only recently been taken. This was all I needed, sitting in a crowded café with people all around. I bowed my head, and pulled my hood up, trying to look inconspicuous while the rest of the story played out. Perhaps I shouldn't have done that, as I couldn't have made myself look guiltier if I had tried.

When I looked up again, I knew I was in trouble.

Not everyone had been paying attention to the TV. There were a lot of young families in the café and most of the parents were far too busy trying to keep their children under control and getting them to eat to watch television.

But as I turned and looked around, I saw the waitress who had served me leaning in close to another woman at the till, whispering something into her ear. Both of them turned to look at me.

Had they seen? They must have. Had anyone else? I looked around the room, catching the eye of an elderly couple at the next table that had been enjoying the pensioner lunchtime special. Both were looking at me.

Glancing back to the till, I could see the woman there tapping her phone screen, then holding it to her ear. Calling the police?

What I did next probably wasn't the wisest move, but I was panicking and just flipped. If the pensioners and the staff had any lingering doubts over whether I was or wasn't the woman on TV, they were about to be swiftly dispelled.

"Had a good look, have you?" I snapped at the old couple as I leapt out of my chair. I needed to get out of this place and fast. I ran for the door, knocking over some kid's pushchair which was blocking the aisle in the process. I didn't bother apologising – the kid wasn't in it, after all: he was in a high chair. Why couldn't people fold the damned things up when they weren't using them?

Nobody tried to stop me as I made my exit, in fact, they didn't even shout after me about the bill. Perhaps they didn't fancy tackling a suspected murderess. So that meant I hadn't paid for my food, so that was stealing to add to my ever-mounting charge sheet.

In just a few seconds, I was out through the door and running down the High Street, not looking back and not sure what to do next.

There was a bus stop a hundred yards or so down the road, and the last person was just getting onto the bus. I ran for the bus and hopped on, without even looking to see where it was going. At least it made my running look less suspicious – after all, people run for buses all the time.

"Where to, love?" asked the driver, in a Scouse accent. At any other time, I would have been glad to encounter a fellow Scouser, but not today. I didn't want to prolong the conversation any longer than necessary or give away any clues as to my origins. I'm not sure if the police would include "Scouse accent" in any description going around about me, but I wasn't taking any risks.

Toning down my accent so he wouldn't clock where I was from, I said.

"I don't know. Where does this bus go?"

As soon as I had said it, I knew it was the wrong thing to say.

"Cheltenham," he replied, looking at me quizzically and then adding, "You know, most people normally know where they want to go when they get on a bus."

"Cheltenham is it, then," I replied.

The bus was packed and I had to walk to the back to find a seat. As I did so, I scanned the passengers, looking for any sign that they recognised me from the news. One or two looked up at me as I passed but there was no hint of recognition. Most were too engrossed in what they were doing – either fiddling around on their phones or away in their own little worlds, courtesy of their headphones.

I was safe – for the moment – but my relief was not to last long. Someone must have followed me out of the café and seen me get on the bus.

When I arrived at the bus station in Cheltenham, the police were waiting for me.

Chapter Eleven
2014

It was 4pm in the afternoon on New Year's Eve and I was stretched out by the pool at a hotel in Gran Canaria, soaking up the gorgeous afternoon sunshine. Tomorrow, it would be my 29th birthday.

Roughly a week had passed in my own personal timeline since the traumatic events surrounding Gary's death and I was now a further four years back in the past. Still feeling awful about what happened, I consoled myself with the thought that in this time, he was still alive.

I had even sent him a text message just to make sure, which was illogical because of course he would be, but it eased my troubled mind. Whilst the traumatic events of that awful day were printed indelibly on my mind, they simply hadn't happened yet, belonging as they did to only one possible future. Perhaps they never would.

I had well and truly learnt my lesson as far as Rob was concerned and had spent my last few trips getting as far away from him and Oxford as possible.

After I had been arrested by the police in Cheltenham, I was taken to the station, checked in, and put in an interview room. They read me my rights at which point I asked for a solicitor to be present. I was just stalling for time really, waiting for 3am to come round when I could be the first person in history to escape police custody by being whisked out of the station into the time vortex.

My solicitor, a bored-looking man in his late thirties called Colin, advised me to say nothing in response to their questions. He didn't seem to want to be there any more than I did, looking every inch a man who would rather be at home watching the telly.

In the end, the two police officers interviewing me became frustrated at my lack of responses and sent me down to the cells for the night. As they did so, they warned me that if I didn't start talking by the morning, I'd be charged with murder.

That's what they thought. It was the first, and hopefully the last, night I would ever spend in a police station in my life. The cell was pretty basic, just a small, square room with a single bunk next to the wall. Unlike cells I had seen on TV, the toilet was in a separate en suite area and even had a seat! I had stayed in worse youth hostels when I had been trekking around Australia during my gap year.

The room service was efficient if the quality of the food left a little to be desired. It consisted of a couple of greasy sausages and some mash in a plastic tray. The whole thing reminded me of an airline meal, right down to the plastic cutlery which was presumably to stop me from self-harming. Sadly there was no wine on offer, as I could have really done with some after the two days I had just had.

Perhaps being arrested had been a blessing. At least I had somewhere warm and dry to spend the night – well, the first half of the night, anyway. The small, basic mattress was surprisingly comfortable and I soon curled up and went to sleep.

The next thing I knew, I was in the nurses' office back at the hospital, sitting with Tessa, my nursing friend with a weakness for food. True to form, she was busy munching her way through a box of mince pies.

"Do you want one, Amy?" she asked. "I don't think I can manage all six."

"Just the one, then," I replied, relieved to be back in such familiar and safe surroundings. I took one and pecked at it daintily while she wolfed them down like there was no tomorrow. She wasn't looking as big as I was used to seeing her, having gained weight as the years had gone by. It wasn't difficult to see why when she was carrying on like this.

"You want to take it easy on those," I admonished gently. "Do you know how many calories they have? It's a moment on the lips, but a lifetime on the hips."

That had been one of my mother's favourite sayings.

"I know. I'm going on a diet for New Year," she pronounced.

I knew she wouldn't stick to it, she never did. There was no point in me saying any more. I needed to get moving if I was going to make the most of my travel plans.

I reached into my bag and took out my latest mobile phone, a Samsung Galaxy S8. It was December 2018 and the S9 had been out nearly a year by now, but I remember being stuck on a two-year contract so couldn't upgrade yet.

I could almost chart my trip back through time by my mobile phones, which were downgrading year by year. How much longer would I have a smartphone? It was 2018 now, so a few more years, I guessed. The further I went back in time, the fewer things I would be able to do using my phone – this was something I needed to prepare for.

What I needed to do now was come up with a convincing reason why I was about to duck out of work in the middle of a shift.

"Oh, what's this?" I said as I unlocked my phone, doing my best to act all surprised. "I've got several missed calls and texts."

Putting on an overly dramatic voice, I reacted, "Oh my God! It's my grandma. She's had a heart attack at her home and been taken into hospital."

"Here?" asked Tessa.

"No," I replied, thinking on my feet, "in Banbury, at the Horton. I must go to her. Can you cover for me?"

"Of course," said Tessa. "You must go. Don't worry, I'll handle things here."

Not for the first time I wondered if I might have succeeded at an acting career, as Tessa had swallowed this latest pile of bullshit almost as effectively as her box of mince pies. The truth was, all of my grandparents had died over a decade before, but she wasn't to know that. The lie got me neatly out of the hospital without the need for any further explanations.

I went straight home, sneaking in quietly in the hope that I wouldn't wake Rob. The thought had crossed my mind that, with me on nights, Emma might be there and I really didn't want to go through all that again.

There was an empty wine bottle in the kitchen with just one glass next to it so it looked like he hadn't had company. If he had drunk the whole bottle on his own, then he would also hopefully be dead to the world.

He certainly was, and I could hear his snoring from halfway up the stairs, even though the bedroom door was shut. His snoring was always worse when he was drinking and as I tiptoed into our room to get my passport, I could see he was dead to the world.

Clearly, he wasn't going to wake up anytime soon, so I took the chance to grab an overnight bag, stuff in some summer clothes, basic toiletries and a swimming costume, and off I went, not forgetting the most important item of all, my passport.

I knew buses ran to Heathrow and Gatwick from Oxford pretty much 24/7, conveniently passing right through St Clement's. By 5.00am I was already on the M40 and heading for the airport. I had decided to go to Heathrow, as I felt that it would offer me a wider choice of destinations.

How easy would it be to get a flight at this time of the morning without pre-booking? It was bound to be expensive, but that was irrelevant. I didn't need to shop around to try and get the best deal. I just needed to get on a plane and get somewhere hot, even if it cost thousands. Perhaps I could even upgrade myself to business or first class. I had never had that luxury before.

My main worry was that they wouldn't take a booking on the spot for the next flight somewhere. With everyone booking everything online these days, was it even still possible to turn up at an airport and book a flight at the desk? Fortunately, even though I arrived early, I was able to find a counter open with one of the big national airlines.

Amazingly, less than four hours after leaving Oxford, I was on a flight to, of all places, Florida. I couldn't believe how easy it had been. The only worrying moment was at airport security where they had given me a good checking-over.

I was slightly worried at that point that I might be in trouble, bearing in mind my recent spell as a fugitive from the police, but again that was all paranoia. No one could be looking for me now.

Perhaps it was just standard procedure to check anyone booking last-minute flights. Security at airports was very tight during this period after a number of terrorist incidents in the early years of the century.

Despite the flight taking nine hours, it was still only early afternoon when I arrived in Orlando, local time. I still had the best part of two days to enjoy this place, somewhere I had always wanted to go. When I was little, my dad had always promised he would bring me here one day, but he fell on hard times after my parents divorced, and it remained a dream – until now.

I hired a car at the airport and drove straight to Walt Disney World resort where I spent the rest of the afternoon. I didn't have anywhere to stay for the night booked, but what did that matter? This was America. When I left the park, I drove until, to my delight, I found an old-fashioned motel, which looked exactly like the ones I had seen in the movies.

Just along from the motel was a similarly nostalgic diner, all decked out with a 1950s theme. I ate there, a huge hamburger with fries and a shake before moving on to the bar next door to celebrate the New Year, American style.

I could barely keep my eyes open until midnight, bearing in mind the time difference between Florida and the UK, and as soon as the hour had passed I went straight back to the motel and crashed out. I had enjoyed a wonderful evening, fully living the American Dream.

The following day I was up very early, again thanks to the time difference, and was away from the motel before 9am. I spent that day at Universal Studios, where even with the full day at my disposal I didn't have time to do everything the park had to offer. I would have liked to have done more, but I just ran out of time.

I didn't bother booking myself into a motel that night because I knew that I would be leaving before the end of the evening. Sure enough, at just 10pm local time, I was whisked away, back to the UK and the early hours of New Year's Eve 2017.

I was in bed this time, as I discovered when I woke up at 5.15am needing to go to the toilet. Although I felt tired, I wasn't going to waste any time sleeping, so I got myself up and dressed, packing my bag just as I had before. In less than an hour I was once again on the bus, Heathrow-bound.

Rather than trust to luck what might be available at the airport, I decided to try and plan ahead a little this time. With phone in hand, I got online while I was on the bus, managing to secure a last-minute flight and hotel deal in Dubai departing that morning. I had wanted winter sunshine and I was certainly going to the right place.

Dubai was fantastic, what little I saw of it. I never left the hotel during the two days I was there. I spent the first evening eating, drinking and checking out the fabulous entertainment the hotel had to offer. Then the next day, I spent the entire day by the pool just revelling in the sensation of the hot Middle Eastern sun on my skin.

I did absolutely nothing that day but was it wasted? Not in my opinion – I was enjoying some much-needed recuperation.

The following year I decided to stay in the UK and go down to London for the fireworks. It was something else on my bucket list that I had never got around to doing but had the opportunity to do now with all the extra New Years at my disposal.

Police were advising people not to travel without a ticket but I soon sorted that out the same way I had got the ticket for *Fever*. I offered to pay four times face value on Facebook, and the offers came flooding in.

Seeing 2017 in by the banks of the Thames was an awesome experience, so much so that I decided to up my game even further the following year. London celebrations were great but I had something even bigger in mind.

Thus, on New Year's Eve 2015, I made my way to New York for what turned out to be one of the most amazing nights of my whole life. Packed into Times Square with hundreds of thousands of others, I partied like never before. Probably even more than Prince had when he sang about partying like it was 1999. It was freezing but I didn't care.

The celebrations went on all evening, to a backdrop of music from some of America's finest DJs. Just before midnight, Jessie J came on to perform a cover of John Lennon's "Imagine", then with just a minute to go, a large, glowing ball descended onto the top of the Times Tower, which is to America at New Year what Big Ben is to the UK.

The accompanying light show was dazzling, with the tower itself lit up like a Christmas tree. The atmosphere was indescribable, like nothing I had experienced before. All those years of hating New Year's Eve were washed away that night. London and Big Ben were great, but nothing could compare to New York.

I wasn't even with anyone but that didn't matter as I enjoyed the company of the revellers all around me, bound together by our shared experience. The party continued long into the night and I found myself chatting to anyone and everyone. I even got a snog off a handsome stranger next to me in the crowd just before we did "Auld Lang Syne".

All in all, it was a pretty cool way to celebrate my 30th birthday.

I smiled as I lie now on my sunbed in my latest destination, an all-inclusive resort in Playa del Inglés, thinking back over the memories of that night, just two days ago. I had turned thirty that day, but now it seemed I would never be that age again.

I looked down at my body, stretched out on the sunbed, clad in just a skimpy bikini. It was a noticeably younger body now. My skin had grown smoother and suppler, my tummy was flatter and my boobs were firmer.

My own personal fountain of youth was making me look better and better but this double-edged sword was going to come back and bite me soon. Now aged twenty-nine, and losing a year every two days, I knew I had less than two months left.

If only this could stop now. I would be happy to stay at this age. I'd have another decade of life, my whole thirties, in front of me, and could do so much more with those ten years than I had.

It was no good thinking like that. There was nothing I could do to stop what was happening. I had tried with the letter to Professor Hamilton but unsurprisingly, that had gone unanswered. Had I ever really expected a reply? Not really. I just had to make the best of what I had.

In reality, I didn't even have two full months left. In terms of my adult life, it was less than a month. Once I became a child, I wouldn't be able to go off jet-setting like I had. I would be a minor, with no money, no passport, and under the jurisdiction of my parents.

My parents – how much was I looking forward to seeing them again? It wouldn't be long now.

Chapter Twelve
2011

A day that I had been in two minds about had arrived.

I had mulled long and hard over how I should handle New Year's Eve 2011. That had been the date of that fateful first meeting with Rob and Gary, the outcome of which was to shape my entire future.

At the time I was living alone in a rented council house off the Iffley Road. It had been my family home for over fifteen years, ever since my mother had become a single parent and sought help from the local authority.

For the last seven years, I had lived there on and off but had been in permanent residence for the past year. I would not be there much longer. My mother died in 2011 and I had no desire to stay in the house alone. The austerity-obsessed government of the time was talking about all sorts of penalties for underoccupancy of council properties, including a so-called bedroom tax.

Quite how that would affect me, I wasn't sure, but it seemed morally wrong to stay in a large house if a family could use it. But where was I going to go? Buying a place on my nurse's salary was out of the question in Oxford and private rent was equally unaffordable.

Thankfully, meeting Rob solved that problem when he asked me to move in with him. I hadn't considered the possibility at the time that I might end up in exactly the same boat nine years down the line, but who does? No matter how badly a relationship breaks down, most of us idealistically believe it will last forever at the start when we are in the first flush of love. Otherwise, why would we bother?

So here I was, waking up at twenty-five years old in the room where I had spent my teenage years. Any casual observer might be under the impression a teenager still lived in the room, as I hadn't done anything to update it for years. There was a reason for this. I hadn't seen it as a permanent home, more of a bolt-hole which I came back to from time to time due to circumstances. In an ideal world, I would have been settled elsewhere by now.

The paint was faded and peeling in the places where it could be seen. Most of the walls were covered up with rock posters, from Nirvana to Oasis. My room was almost like a shrine to the 1990s music scene.

As for my bed, that was only a single. I had thought about buying a double, but somehow that didn't seem quite right in my mother's house and didn't fit in with my "temporary residence" status. There was a double bed in my mother's room, which she had died in and I couldn't face moving in there.

The single bed meant my sexual encounters in this room had been very few and far between, most confined to my teenage years. That didn't mean I'd had a non-existent sex life, merely that most of it had taken place elsewhere.

Although I was living here now, I had come and gone a lot between the ages of eighteen and twenty-five. As well as time at university doing my nursing degree, I had also spent a great deal of time abroad, both travelling and working.

I had moved back in with my mother full-time just under a year ago to nurse her through the illness that eventually killed her. Fifty-nine had been no age to die, though my father had been even younger.

Now I was alone and contemplating what to do with the day ahead of me. Was I going to relive that first meeting with

Rob and Gary or avoid it? I knew that I couldn't resist it – out of fascination more than anything.

As if on cue, my phone beeped, and I picked it up to find a text from Kelly.

Can't wait for tonight, it's going to be awesome. Bet I pull before you x

Her bubbly, fun, text reminded me of what a laugh going out with her used to be. I wondered if she remembered in the years to come when she became so utterly domesticated and boring, how different she had once been.

Well, she wasn't going to pull first this time. My mind was made up. I still had no idea if anything I did here changed the future but if it did, then I was going to do my utmost to make it happen. I wasn't doing it purely for selfish reasons either. There was Gary to think about. Changing things now would very probably save his life several years from now. Here was a chance to clean up the mess I had made that day.

It was difficult for me to remember the precise details of everything that had happened on that night because, from my starting point, it was now thirteen years ago. Every year I went back in time, the memories grew more and more hazy.

One thing I could remember with certainty about this night was that we had met the boys in O'Neill's on George Street. I knew that hadn't been the pub we had started in or anywhere else we had been, so I needed to text Kelly back to find out.

Remind me, when & where are we meeting again?

The reply came back swiftly:

In The Crown, 6.30! Don't be late!

That's right: we were meeting in one of my old stomping grounds. It had always been a favourite, a good, traditional pub down the alley next to McDonald's, where crowds of foreign tourists always seemed to gather. Fighting my way through them was always worth it because The Crown was a great little hideaway, right in the centre of town.

Dutifully, I was there at 6.30pm, looking my best, which by my 2025 standards was a million dollars. My body was getting better every day and now, at the age of 25, I was at my absolute peak – fully developed with not a hint of ageing.

I am pretty confident I also looked better than I had the first time around on this night out. I had spent the day shopping for clothes, coming back this time with a £300 dress from Debenhams, plus new shoes and a bag.

I had also spent a further £90 getting my hair and nails done in a swanky salon down the High Street. I would not have been able to afford any of that last time.

If I was expecting compliments from Kelly on meeting up, I was to be disappointed. Unlike Phoebe and Lily who had been thrilled to see me in the dress from the Covered Market, Kelly's reaction was the complete opposite. She was one of those who wanted to be queen bee, and I could see right away her disapproval at me upstaging her.

"Nice dress," she said begrudgingly as we met outside the pub, which was her sole comment on my outfit. She was heavily tarted up for a night on the pull. She had pouting red lips where she had gone overboard with the lipstick and way too much makeup.

She was wearing the same short, all-red outfit I remembered she always referred to as her pulling gear. The tight, red cotton hugged her slender behind, accentuating its shape whilst her curly, flame-red hair, which matched her dress, flowed down around her shoulders.

Kelly had a great figure. She had always been a good few pounds lighter than me and didn't let me forget it, slipping in the odd reference now and again.

Seeing her again and remembering all that had subsequently happened made me question how good a friend she ever really was. Her barely veiled displeasure at seeing how good I looked was typical of her. She was determined to be the prettiest, slimmest and sexiest. That way she would always get first pick of the men.

It was strange that this hadn't bothered me so much at the time anywhere near as much as it bothered me now. Perhaps I hadn't noticed so much in these youthful, more naïve times. Well, I was noticing now, and she wasn't going to get the upper hand over me tonight.

"Come on, let's get to the bar," I said impatiently. I needed to be bold tonight and a little Dutch courage could only help.

"Cocktails?" I suggested.

"Go for it," she replied.

A couple of Tequila Sunrises later, we headed down Cornmarket Street and into George Street. We had tickets for a club which I had no recollection of attending, but that didn't open until 10pm. It was only 8.30pm now, and not wanting to pre-empt anything, I asked Kelly where we should go, curious to see if she would steer us towards our destiny.

"A lot of the places are ticket-only tonight," she replied, "but I am pretty sure O'Neill's isn't."

"Let's try there, then," I replied, allowing things to proceed along their natural course.

The place was rammed, largely with groups of single men and women and there were a lot more men than women. It was prime pulling potential. Of course, I already knew what was to come – Kelly didn't.

"There's some talent in here tonight," remarked Kelly, "and a good male-to-female ratio! I'm definitely getting some tonight."

She was such a tart in this era. It was strange seeing how different she was, knowing how much she would change. It would be just a few short years before she would put all of this behind her, settle down, and become incredibly dull, ultimately disowning me over my casual ADHD joke on Facebook.

I wonder if settling down had been what she had really wanted, or whether it was just something that happened to her. What changes would she make if she had her chance over again? Would she choose the same path?

I scanned the room, trying to spot Rob and Gary, but it was extremely crowded. All I could remember for certain is that we had first met them at the bar.

"My round," proclaimed Kelly. "What are you having?"

"Tell you what, why don't I get these?" I suggested. "You see if you can find us a table."

I needed to take any opportunity to try and engineer things in my favour, and it was therefore essential I got to the bar before she did.

"Not much chance of getting a seat in here," she replied. "And who wants to sit down anyway? Come on, let's get some drinks." And grabbing my hand to drag me through the crowd, she made a beeline for the bar.

This wasn't ideal. If I let her find Rob and Gary before I did, my plans could go up in smoke. I had just one advantage – I knew who I was looking for and she didn't. I needed to make that edge count.

Fighting our way through to the bar wasn't easy. The throng of people jostling for drinks was three-deep and manoeuvring our way to the front line was a challenge. When we did, we found that getting there was half the battle – getting served in turn was quite another.

A lot of the traditional British etiquette about queue jumping seemed to go out of the window when it came to getting drinks in crowded pubs. We just had to hope they had experienced staff on tonight who knew what the pecking order was when it came to serving people. That wasn't the case in all pubs.

Fortunately, the team behind the bar seemed to know what they were doing, ignoring the fat man who had rudely squashed into the right of me whilst waving a twenty-pound note in the direction of the barmaid. As if that was going to get him served any quicker! When I served behind the bar at college for a term, those idiots always went straight to the back of the queue.

Kelly was on my left and had attracted the attention of a barmaid who had done a grand job of pretending not to see the money-waving bloater next to me. Thank goodness she had. I needed to get away from him as soon as possible. The sweet, sickly stench of his cheap aftershave was overpowering in my nostrils.

Clearly, he had worked up a sweat hauling his bulky frame up to the bar because I could smell that, too. I really hoped he didn't suffer from flatulence, as that would be the icing on a seriously unappetising cake. In my haste to get out of there fast, I had temporarily forgotten all about Gary and Rob.

Kelly had ordered two more cocktails, but just as she was about to pay, I heard a very familiar voice speak from her other side. The music was loud, The Pogues version of "The Irish Rover" blaring in the background, but even over that, I still recognised his voice instantly.

"Can I get those, love?" said Gary.

He was right next to her on the other side. This was a bad start because she was in pole position. This was exactly as it had happened before. Was I powerless to change things? Was the future preordained?

No, that could not be the case. If it was, how come I had managed to cause him to get killed the last time we had met? I could still turn this around, even though the opening exchange had gone against me. Kelly had already turned to accept his offer, eyeing him with a flirty glance. As for Rob, he was on Gary's other side, almost out of view.

There was nothing else for it. I was going to have to do something drastic. Fat boy's B.O. next to me was getting on my tits, so I felt no qualms about what I did next.

As soon as I had my drink in my hand, I leaned back into him, and then quickly lurched forward, chucking my entire Tequila Sunrise all over Kelly.

She shrieked, "For fuck's sake, Amy, what are you doing?!" She was drenched. It was amazing how much mess just one drink could make. I had only intended to get it on her dress but it had gone all over her face and hair, too, completely messing her up.

"Oh God, Kelly, I'm so sorry. It was this twat here, he just barged into me."

"What?" exclaimed the fat man, turning to look at me for the first time, eyeing me in my dress with his leery little eyes as he did so. What a pig. I thought he was going to deny it, but he didn't. Perhaps he thought he might get in my knickers if he took the blame. Dream on!

"I'm really sorry," he said. "Let me buy you another."

"Never mind that, I'm fucking soaked!" shouted Kelly. Queen bees don't handle these sorts of situations well and I was enjoying her discomfort immensely. I needed to take care not to show that, though.

"Calm down," I said, instantly wishing I hadn't. I had learnt the hard way at school as a Scouser never to use this

153

phrase, as everyone took the piss. "It'll be alright, just go to the toilets and dry off."

Grumbling, she took a towel kindly offered by the barmaid who had been serving us and headed off to the toilets. The bumbling idiot next to me was blathering on, full of apology. As soon as I had the replacement drinks from him, I turned the other way, towards Gary and Rob who had been watching this whole display with amused detachment.

"Is your friend going to be OK?" asked Rob.

It was the first time I had heard him speak and he seemed a lot quieter and much less confident than I remembered from this night. Looking at the two of them side by side, there was no denying that I fancied Gary more. So why had I gone with Rob that night? Had I been simply settling for the silver medal because Kelly had claimed the first prize? If so, it was a pretty poor starting point to base the next nine years of my life on.

It didn't say much for me as a person, did it? Without realising it at the time, I had fallen into a trap that I think many people do. Instead of taking the time to pick the right person to have a relationship with, I had just settled for the first person who came along.

"She'll be fine," I said. "She'll be back in a minute."

"Shall we get away from the bar before there are any more mishaps?" suggested Gary. It was a fair question. It was getting a bit like a rugby scrum where we were standing and the replacement drinks I was holding were definitely in peril.

Concurring, and ignoring the fat man who was still standing next to me, I took a firm hold of both my and Kelly's new drinks. Leaving our fat friend behind us, the three of us vacated our spots at the bar, briefly leaving a void that was filled as swiftly as water rushing through a burst dam.

154

Now we were out in the open, we all had a better view of each other. Looking me up and down in my newly acquired outfit, Gary remarked, "You look stunning in that dress."

It didn't sound like a chat-up line but completely genuine and I took the compliment gratefully. I don't recall him saying anything like that before, but on the previous occasion this night had played out, I had just been wearing some cheap top from Dorothy Perkins.

"Quick, grab this table," said Rob, as a group of four blokes got up to leave. I'm pretty sure it wasn't the same table we had the previous time, as this one was by the window. The added time spent at the bar was already causing the timeline to deviate. The choice of table was a minor change, one that would have no long-term effect on the timeline, but now it was time to bring about a major change.

Kelly returned ten minutes later, chastened and patched up, but still with an amusingly obvious wet patch on her right breast. By then, I had ensured that the battle lines had been well and truly drawn in my favour. This time it was me at the end of the table with Gary next to me, then Rob. I had ensured that there was only one place she could fit into this arrangement and that was on the other side of Rob.

From then on it was plain sailing. I didn't spend the night alone, waking up on New Year's Day with Gary in his flat. A second bout of passion with him had been a welcome bonus from my night's work, and thankfully this time it was all legit and above board. We were both single at this time so no one was going to stumble upon us, go into a rage, and bring about an improbable death armed with nothing more than a small vegetable knife.

In many ways, it was a good deal more satisfying than last time. We were both almost a decade younger, fitter and with more energy, and I felt the earth move more times that night than I ever had with Rob. I wondered what sort of night Kelly had had with him, inevitably going back to his place as she had. I am willing to bet she wouldn't have enjoyed herself as much as I had.

Where would Gary and I go from here? It was impossible to say. If I was opening up a new timeline with each trip back in time, then maybe this might be one where he and I had ended up living happily ever after. Who knows, we might even have had kids.

I had been a bit mercenary in getting what I wanted, blaming the fat man for the drink spillage and treading on Kelly's toes. But I didn't feel guilty about either. The fat man, he had been rude and arrogant, waving his money at the bar staff. He had also offended me with his terrible taste in aftershave and his B.O.

As for Kelly, well, she had never been much more than a fair-weather friend and I saw her now for what she was. The knowledge that she was going to drop me faster than a ton of bricks within a couple of years when I was no longer of any interest to her was more than enough justification for my behaviour. I had almost got a kick out of messing up her hair and clothes, even though I had vowed not to use my time-travelling powers for any more revenge tactics.

Just this once, it had been worth it.

Now it was time to move on. I was heading back towards the noughties and some of the most difficult days of my life lay ahead.

Chapter Thirteen
2010

If I had been apprehensive about the previous New Year, I was positively dreading this one.

2011 had been a dark year. Something happened that I was powerless to prevent at the time, and I would still be unable to do anything about it at this particular point in time. Further back in time perhaps I might have a chance, but on this date, it was already far too late.

It was the year that my mother had died, just a few days short of the milestone that would have been her fiftieth birthday. She hadn't been killed in a car crash or any other external influence. If she had, then I would have the ability to warn her. But what was going to kill her was already irreversible by now.

It wasn't a hereditary illness or contagion that was to take her, but a misadventure of her own making. Quite simply, and very sadly, she had drunk herself to death. Diagnosed with the advanced stages of liver cancer in January, she was dead less than three months later.

I was dreading this trip because, unlike many of my birthdays, I remembered in great clarity what had happened that year. I knew what was coming, and I had scant hope that I was going to be able to do anything about it, but I had to at least try.

Why did my mother drink so much in her later years? She hadn't always been an alcoholic. Like most young people of her generation, she had partied hard in her youth, drinking and smoking with her friends. She had gone to an all-girls school in Oxford and had often told me tales of what she and her friends had got up to. They used to go out at lunchtime for a sneaky snakebite at a pub close to the school that turned a blind eye to underage drinking.

This was back in the 1970s when things were a lot more lax in that area. Such behaviour was almost seen as a rite of passage, as was buying single Silk Cut cigarettes from the man in the sweetshop at 5p a time.

Then, in the early 1980s, she met my dad who had come down from Liverpool in search of work due to the chronic unemployment on Merseyside at that time. One thing led to another and before too long she was pregnant with Rachel.

My sister was born in the summer of 1983, by which time our parents had tied the knot, which society still expected in such circumstances at that time. Dad was a plumber by trade, and when offered a job back in Liverpool by a former colleague who had set up his own firm, he jumped at the chance. By the time I was born at the dawning of 1986, the family was firmly settled back up there.

Life was good – for a while, and during my formative years, I had no reason to suspect my mother might have a problem with alcohol. She was certainly no different to anyone else of her generation, enjoying a glass of wine in the evening and having a few in the clubhouse when we used to go on caravan holidays in Prestatyn. I never questioned any of this at the time – it just seemed like normal behaviour. The real problems didn't begin until much later.

As I moved towards the end of the first decade of my life I started to sense that all was not well at home. Mum and Dad had argued like most couples do but towards my tenth birthday, the rows became more and more bitter. It wasn't the case that they just weren't getting on; they had reached a point where they actively seemed to despise each other.

Then one day in the summer holidays, without warning or any proper explanation, my mother packed up a suitcase each for me and Rachel, got us a taxi to Lime Street station, and shipped us off down to Oxford. She said we were going to visit grandparents which we often did. But this time we never came back.

After a couple of years, when the inevitable divorce had been settled, we were allowed to go back up to Liverpool to stay with Dad a few times a year. The full truth about why my parents had split did not come out until many years later. When it did, it was an entirely predictable story.

My father had been having an affair with his mate's wife – the one who had given him the job in his plumbing firm. My mother had caught them both in their bed while Rachel and I had both been at school. He lost more than his marriage that afternoon. When his mate found out, he got sacked as well.

The story of him getting caught in the act came back to haunt me years later. When I caught Rob and Emma at it, I knew how my mother must have felt.

The three of us stayed in my grandparents' home for a while until we managed to get the council house on the Iffley Road. From there, my mother began to rebuild her life. She seemed happy enough to begin with, establishing a new social life once Rachel and I were old enough to be left alone in the late-1990s.

Mum had a few boyfriends back then, but never anything serious. I remember her saying marriage had been a mistake and that she was happy it just being all us girls together. She was adamant that she had no intention of settling down again.

She got a clerical job at the university which she seemed to enjoy and often went out drinking with her colleagues in Oxford after work. Even then the drinking didn't seem like any big deal, particularly since I was out doing it myself by this time and on a much larger scale.

159

Then Rachel died and everything changed. Mum hit the bottle hard. Desperate for help, I called Dad who came down to try and help, the three of us reunited in grief. He seemed genuinely remorseful for his past behaviour and the two of them seemed to be getting on much better than they ever had when we had all lived together in Liverpool.

I even harboured hopes that they might get back together but then came a second, devastating blow that was to put the final nail in the coffin.

Just six months after Rachel's death, Dad dropped down dead of a heart attack, just as he and Mum were on the brink of reconciliation. The two of them had gone to see the recently released *War of the Worlds* movie at the cinema, but in the foyer, he began complaining of chest pains. By the time the ambulance arrived, he was dead.

Grief-stricken, I threw all of my energy into my career, working as many hours as I could. I also went through a promiscuous phase, sleeping with random men in desperate attempts to bring temporary respite from my pain.

For my mother, it was far worse. Whilst I still had youth and energy on my side, she was worn out by it all. Her way of dealing with it was through drink.

I went away a lot, working with the Red Cross abroad, and seeing the world. Every time I came back, Mum had got worse. She lost her job and her friends and began drinking pretty much all day. I tried to help her and discourage her drinking but she became bitter and defensive, lashing out at me as if it was somehow my fault. It was as if I was to blame, just by being the only one of the three of us left alive.

I realise now she was doing it because I was the only one left she could rant at. Maybe I shouldn't have gone away so much and stayed to try and help her, but it was so difficult when she made me feel so unwelcome.

This state of affairs continued for over five years, leading us to where we were today. During that period, she got worse and worse. Several years of serious alcohol abuse on top of a lifetime of drinking took their toll to the extent that, by this New Year, she was in a bad way.

I could see this as soon as I stumbled downstairs, on this dark and dismal winter's morning. I had woken up back in my teenage room again, unchanged since the last time I had seen it, but downstairs I was confronted by a completely different scene.

Last time I had seen the kitchen, in the year after my mother's death, it had been reasonably tidy. Now it was anything but. The sink was full of undone washing up; there were empty takeaway trays lying around, an overflowing ashtray on the kitchen table, and empty bottles everywhere.

It looked like the sort of scene you might expect to find in a kitchen the morning after a party, but it had been a long time since there had been anything to celebrate in this house. This mess was entirely of my mother's making.

There were two empty red wine bottles and a three-quarters finished bottle of Bacardi Spiced Rum on the table. It was perfectly possible she had drunk all of that just the previous day. That's how bad things had got. Of my mother, there was no sign. She must be sleeping it off either in bed or on the sofa, where she frequently crashed out.

What was I going to do? What could I do? Hide all the booze? Tip it down the sink? That wouldn't stop her and would just get me screamed at. It was way too late now, anyway.

Perhaps I could try and talk to her. I remember I had tried in the past without much success, but now I had advance knowledge of exactly what was going to happen, maybe I could get through to her.

161

It was only just getting light outside, and just after 8am according to the kitchen clock. Sweeping away some of the detritus littering the kitchen surfaces, I located the coffee machine and prepared to put together my morning fix. All that caffeine probably wasn't doing me much good, but it was a lot less harmful than what was flowing through my mother's veins.

Once the coffee pot was bubbling away, I got to grips with the business of clearing up the mess my mother had left the kitchen in. I had tackled the dishes and the takeaway boxes when I heard the telltale creak of her footsteps on the stairs. It was early, but then she had probably gone to bed early after she had drunk herself into a stupor, as she did most days.

I remembered my mother looking bad in her final days, but time had taken the edge off my memories of how bad a state she was really in.

She hobbled into the room in a baggy old T-shirt and jeans which were both way too big for her. This wasn't surprising and she had been losing weight continually during that last year, possibly a symptom of the illness inside her.

The clothes looked dishevelled, and I strongly suspected she had not only been wearing them for several days but had also slept in them. Also, even though I was several feet away from her as she entered the room I caught the unmistakable whiff of alcohol.

The skin on her arms and face was dry, almost parchment-like, and there was a yellowish look around her eyes. This was not my mother – not the mother I had grown up with. This was a hollow husk of what she had once been.

Trying not to show any signs of the shock I felt at her appearance, I tried to put on a brave face.

"Morning, Mum," I began. "I've got a pot of coffee on. Would you like some?"

"Amy, you know I can't stand the stuff," she replied, grumpily, as she made a beeline straight for the table, eyes set on the Bacardi bottle.

"How about some breakfast, then?" I suggested, already knowing what the answer would be.

"I'm not hungry," she snapped, reaching for the bottle. I remembered that she rarely ate during the day, existing pretty much on takeaways at night in her later days.

I had to try and say something, even though I knew it would do no good.

"Mum, you really shouldn't be drinking this early in the morning," I began.

"Don't tell me what I can and can't do in my own home, Amy!" she retorted angrily.

She was always like this. Any suggestion that she should cut down on her drinking was met with hostility.

"I'm not, Mum, but think of what it's doing to your health."

She laughed a dark, gallows humour-type of laugh, exposing her rows of blackened, rotting teeth.

"Do you think I care?" she said. "What have I got that's worth living for?"

"You've got me," I replied.

"Yeah, when it suits," she replied. "How long before you bugger off back to Australia or wherever?"

"I'm here for you, Mum," I replied. "I want to help you."

"It's too late to help me," she replied, resignedly. "You'd be better off out of it, living your own life."

Sadly, I knew she was right, but I wasn't giving up. Even if I couldn't do anything today, maybe I could on my next trip. If I could just try and get her to open up, I might be able to discover something I could work with next time.

"Mum, why are you being like this? Is it because of what happened to Rachel?"

Immediately I knew I had said the wrong thing.

"Don't you dare mention her name in this house!" she yelled, her jaundiced eyes blazing. "If she was here, she wouldn't be giving me this grief. Rachel would have understood."

The message was loud and clear. Rachel was better than me. Rachel was her favourite, and it had been the wrong daughter who had died. That was what she was implying.

But I knew that simply wasn't true. She had always treated us equally when Rachel had been alive. The only advantage my sister had over me now was that she wasn't here and I was. Her death had raised her onto a pedestal in my mother's eyes, at a level that I simply couldn't attain whilst still alive.

"Mum, Rachel's gone," I said softly. "Please let me help you." I reached for the bottle, but she snatched it away before I could get hold of it.

"Leave me alone!" she screamed as she removed the lid and upended the bottle into her mouth, glugging it down like there was no tomorrow.

"Mum, stop!" I shouted. I had never seen her drink out of the bottle like this before. Was this her response to my attempted intervention? To just drink even more to spite me? It seemed all I was doing was making things worse.

Suddenly she broke off from downing the rum with a sharp cry of pain. Attempting to place the bottle back on the table, she missed, and it fell to the floor, shattering on the earthenware kitchen tiles.

Bending almost double, her hand went to her right side, just beneath her ribcage as she yelped again in pain.

"Mum, what is it?" I cried, even though I already knew.

She looked up at me with a pleading in her eyes.

"Pain," she said, gasping for breath. "Help me, Amy," she cried.

Although this had happened before, I hadn't expected it to be happening right now. I remember quite clearly that this had happened the following day, on my birthday. She had collapsed in pain just like now, and I had phoned an ambulance and she had been taken into hospital.

Why was it happening now, a day early? Had our row and her subsequent upending of the rum bottle triggered the pain early? Whatever the reason, I had no alternative but to follow the same course of action as before and phone for an ambulance.

A few hours later I was sitting by her hospital bed as she slept. I was in one of the very wards that I would soon be employed in.

I knew that soon a doctor would come round to give me the inevitable news that she had advanced liver cancer. Getting there a day early wasn't going to make one iota of difference. She would never be going home again. From here, it would be a hospice which was where she would end her days.

I had known from the outset that there would be nothing I could do but at least I had confronted the problem with her and got some indication of how she was feeling.

Now I could try again, in the past, when there might still be time to turn things around.

It would be three more years until I got another chance.

Chapter Fourteen
2007

I was back in my bedroom again, three years before my mother's death, wondering if I would be able to get through to her this time.

I had not seen her since that awful day when I had ended up taking her to hospital because I had arrived abroad on both my next two trips back in time.

After I had finished my nursing degree, I decided to work abroad with the Red Cross for a few years before I settled down to work at the hospital. They had been richly rewarding years – hard work, and harrowing at times, but without doubt, they were the best years of my adult life.

On New Year's Eve 2009, I found myself in Indonesia, helping out in the aftermath of a devastating earthquake. There had been a number of disasters in the Asia-Pacific region that year which had led to a strong Red Cross presence in the area. Before arriving in Sumatra, I had been giving aid in the Philippines which had experienced an extremely destructive typhoon.

I had been part of the team deployed to help out with the aid effort. Even though several weeks had passed since the earthquake by the time I arrived in Sumatra, the signs of devastation were everywhere.

My job included everything from dealing with aid deliveries coming in from abroad to helping the locals rebuild their shattered communities.

On New Year's Eve, I found myself in a small fishing village on the Sumatran coast where a Red Cross team was helping to build a new emergency centre to provide temporary shelter for families of the local fishermen.

This was intended not only for use in the current disaster but also to be robust enough to withstand future earthquakes. It was being built on the highest land in the area, which also took into account the risk of associated tsunamis. After what had happened to Rachel, this was a project extremely close to my heart.

I spent the night in the village, celebrating New Year with the locals. Despite the recent disaster, all the villagers were determined to face 2010 with a renewed sense of optimism. Very few could speak English but this didn't matter. We had a shared bond that transcended language. We sang, danced and partied all night around a large bonfire on the beach.

The next day, I travelled to the warehouse in Padang to continue work in coordinating the relief effort.

The following year I found myself in Australia. I wasn't working there, but doing the obligatory backpacker thing, exploring the delights that this huge country had to offer.

This was the year after I had finished my degree when I was combining Red Cross work with travelling. I was in my early twenties at the time and remembered my trip to Australia fondly. The one thing that would have made it better was some more money as I was travelling on the absolute breadline, but I had planned to do something about that.

When I arrived on New Year's Eve, I materialised on Bondi Beach, where I was lying on a towel soaking up the hot Southern Hemisphere sunshine. Just as when I had arrived in Indonesia, this was another welcome respite from the endless drudgery of cold British December days I had been enduring for what seemed like forever.

One feature of being so far from home was that I arrived on these trips in the daytime. In Sumatra, I had been in the middle of building work on the shelter and this time it was already early afternoon, hence the sunbathing. This was infinitely preferable to arriving at night when I would have found myself in the grotty hostel with several other people.

I had no intention of going back to the hostel tonight. I was getting pretty good at planning things by now, and knowing I was going to be in Sydney on this date, I had made preparations to make my stay infinitely more comfortable than before.

One of the things I remembered about Australia was how popular horse racing was over there. Unlike in the UK, where alcohol and betting shops didn't mix, here things were a lot more relaxed. It seemed many pubs had betting facilities on tap along with the beer.

Although horse racing had never been my thing, I had done my homework before the trip and now knew all about the TAB which stood for Totalisator Agency Board. This was the Australian equivalent of our British bookmakers and I was intending to win some tidy sums of money to help my New Year celebrations along a bit.

There were many things I had wanted to do in Sydney but just hadn't had the money. I was fresh out of college, with very little in the way of funds and had been doing casual jobs along the way to keep my trip going. All of that was about to change.

I had gleaned all I could about the Australian system from the internet. All of the results going back years were available in an archive online so I had memorised the results from a couple of the big meetings taking place on the day in question. Much as I was enjoying the feeling of the sun on Bondi Beach, it must already be around 2pm by my calculations, so I needed to get off the beach and into a local TAB office.

I had planned things carefully and didn't go crazy in the first place I visited. It was a bar with a betting shop tacked onto the side. There, I had A$20 on each of the first two winners and then moved on to another bar.

I didn't want to attract too much attention, which wasn't easy, even without backing winners. The punters in the bars were curious who this young English woman was backing horses. It's fair to say, I didn't fit the profile of the average punter.

Over the afternoon, I visited four or five TAB outlets, winning increasing amounts in each. By the end of the day, I had well over A$2000 in brightly coloured notes. That would be enough to substantially upgrade my New Year celebrations.

I booked myself a proper hotel for two nights, which enabled me to rid myself of my backpack which I had been carrying around with me everywhere. Leaving it in the hostel wasn't a good idea. After that, I went on one of my regular shopping sprees to spruce myself up for the evening ahead.

Once I was scrubbed up and suitably attired, no longer looking like a grubby backpacker, I got myself down to the harbour. There I was lucky enough to find a cruise still taking bookings for the evening. I saw in the New Year in style, watching the fireworks over the Opera House after a gorgeous dinner on board the boat.

The dining had been arranged at long tables with no formal seating plan, so I hadn't looked obviously alone and soon made the acquaintance of others along my table. Just as in New York, I ended up having a fantastic time, making me reflect once again that New Year wasn't so bad if you were in the right place to enjoy it.

With plenty of money left, I went sightseeing the next day, doing the Sydney Harbour Bridge Walk, and then dining at the Sydney Tower revolving restaurant. I must have eaten half my body weight in there, taking the opportunity to try all sorts of exotic and local meats I hadn't encountered before.

Both Indonesia and Australia had been once-in-a-lifetime experiences which I had now been fortunate enough to enjoy twice in mine. I definitely made more of both this second time around, leading me to wonder how much better all our lives could have been if we had all been given a second bite of the cherry.

I had certainly been making good use of mine. Perhaps not to begin with, when I was still learning how this worked and making mistakes, but certainly since the wake-up call of what had happened to Gary. I had been having a lot of fun but there was the ever-looming reality that time was running out like sand through an hourglass. I now had only a few years left as an adult.

Now it was the year before Australia and I was back at home, three years now before my mother's death. Perhaps if I could stop her drinking now, it would be in time to save her.

I got up, got dressed and made my way downstairs. My room had looked the same as ever, but there were notable changes in the rest of the house since my last visit. The most obvious of these was that it was much cleaner and tidier. It was not a show home by any means, but far from the rank state, it had been the last time I had been there. That meant she hadn't totally given up yet. That gave me hope.

There was no sign of my mother, but some evidence she had been around this morning. There was an empty coffee cup and a small, crumb-covered plate and butter knife next to the sink. This was also an encouraging sign. At least she was still eating and drinking properly at this time and hadn't yet reached the alcohol-for-breakfast stage.

Even so, there was evidence of the previous evening's drinking. On the kitchen surface next to the sink was an empty wine glass and two empty wine bottles next to it. Whether or not she had drunk all of that the previous night, I had no idea, but I wouldn't have put it past her. At least there were no spirits – or none that I could see, anyway.

171

I glanced across at the calendar, which showed that it was Monday, so she had probably gone to work. If I remembered rightly, she still had her job at this time but probably not for much longer. Around this time she had become so unreliable that the college had sacked her.

Losing her job had been the tipping point that had seen her descend into all-day drinking. At least while she still had the job there was some structure to give her a semblance of normality. If I could stop her drinking before that happened, maybe there was still hope. I had two days to try and convince her.

But to do that, I first had to find her, and she proved to be remarkably elusive. I tried ringing and texting her mobile from my Nokia, but drew a blank there, too. I didn't want to go out in case I missed her, so I stayed at home all day, assuming she would be home straight after work. Unfortunately, that was not the case. I waited and waited until long after dark, but there was no sign.

I made good use of my time while I was waiting. I had come to the conclusion that a little future knowledge could come in very useful in my later trips, so I spent most of the day on the internet using the laughably slow laptop in my bedroom.

I went through every year from 1990 onwards, reading, writing down and memorising key facts about every year. Then I reread it again and again, hoping as much as possible would stick.

It was well into the evening by the time I finished and there was still no sign of her. What if she didn't come back at all? It was New Year, after all – she may have gone straight out to a party after work. I tried to remember, but it was pointless – I couldn't remember exactly what had happened in this particular year. It was a nondescript one, not like an Australia or a Sumatra which stuck in the mind.

Social media was no help either. I no longer had a smartphone – my Nokia had only the most basic of internet facilities. I did have Facebook on the laptop, but it was an extremely primitive-looking version and I had only recently joined. I had a grand total of seventeen friends and my mother was not one of them.

This backwards nature of technology was seriously beginning to irk me. Stuck at home for the evening, I decided I may as well stay in and watch the telly, but we didn't even have a decent TV anymore, just this great big silver/grey box, on which the standard definition picture quality was seriously lacking by the standards I was used to.

By the time Jools Holland came on, I had pretty much written off any hope of having a decent conversation with my mother tonight. Even if she did come in before I went to bed, she was bound to be drunk and I needed her to be sober if I was to have any hope of getting through to her.

Drunk is exactly what she was when she rolled in at 2am as I was struggling to keep my eyes open. Even worse, she wasn't alone. She had dragged some dodgy-looking geezer from the pub back with her.

I had never seen this man before, but I only had to take one look at him to see he was a waste of space. He seemed to be trying to cultivate some sort of ageing rockstar look, with long, greasy hair tied into a ponytail and a faded, old denim jacket. Even this far back in my past, his attire was still at least a decade, possibly two, past being fashionable. His outfit was rounded out by matching jeans, and a scuffed old pair of Doc Martens.

As for his appearance, he was unshaven and unkempt, but still fairly fresh-faced underneath the two-day-old stubble. I was guessing he wasn't as old as his clothes suggested and probably closer to my age than my mother's.

"Oh Amy," gushed my mother, "I wasn't expecting you to be home. I thought you were at a party tonight."

She was slurring and unsteady on her feet.

"Who's this?" I asked, gesturing at the denim-clad loser next to her.

"Oh, this is Andy," she said. "I met him at the pub tonight. He used to be a rockstar, didn't you, Andy?"

"I did," replied her drunken friend in an equally inebriated tone. "I've been on TV and everything."

"Yes, he's been telling me all about it," she said. "I've invited him back for a nightcap."

"So I see," I said, knowing full well what the nightcap would lead to. This sort of thing had happened several times in those final years. I decided to leave them to it and try again in the morning.

"Well, I'm off to bed," I said, trying to hide my disgust. "Have fun."

I got out of there sharpish as the two of them staggered into the kitchen in search of more booze. I was quite disgusted by what I had just seen. My forty-six-year-old mother with some loser from the pub who was almost young enough to be her son was not a pretty sight.

When I heard laughter and heavy footsteps on the stairs, I grabbed my iPod classic and turned it up to full volume. Hearing Phoebe having sex through the walls in our flat was one thing – the thought of my mother with this waster was quite another.

Thankfully, when I got up late the following morning, there was no sign of him. Mercifully, she had sent him on his way and was now sitting in the kitchen nursing a coffee. She was looking seriously the worse for wear, but as least she hadn't started on the booze – yet.

"Morning, Amy," she began. "Want some coffee?"

She hadn't given any indication she was going to mention last night, so it looked like it was up to me to bring it up.

"Who the hell was that last night, Mum?"

"Don't judge me, Amy," she snapped, clearly spoiling for a row. This was a bad start. I had got her on the offensive with my first remark. Why was I so crap at handling these things?

"I'm not," I replied. "But seriously, how old was he?"

"He's thirty, for your information," she said. "That's what he said anyway, not that it matters."

"That's sick," I said, and before I could stop myself, I blurted out another unwise choice of phrase. "Don't you think that makes him seem a bit desperate?"

"Why, because he wants an old slapper like me?!" she shouted. "Who the hell do you think you are, Amy? It's my business what I do, nobody else's."

"Look, Mum," I said, trying to be reconciliatory. "I'm worried about you. You're drinking an awful lot these days and bringing all sorts back to the house."

"Who's the parent here, me or you?" she demanded. "Let's get one thing clear right away. You don't tell me what to do, OK? I tell you. And besides, Andy isn't all sorts – he's a nice guy."

I wanted to retort with the observation that he was a total loser but managed to restrain myself. I had messed this up enough already.

"OK, I'm sorry," I said. "Maybe I misjudged him. But I'm really worried about how much you've been drinking since Rachel…"

She cut me off before I could finish, yelling, "Don't you dare bring her into this!"

This was not going well at all. It was in danger of turning into a carbon copy of the conversation we had already had three years in the future. I was getting nowhere and it was time to change tack. There was nothing else for it, I was going to have to try and tell her the truth.

"I'm sorry," I said, "but I've got something important to tell you."

"Like what?" she said scornfully as if I couldn't possibly have anything to say that she would be interested in.

There was no point messing around with any convoluted explanations about how I had come to be where I was, I just needed to get it out, concisely, before she interrupted me again.

"Mum, if you don't stop drinking, you are going to die. I've travelled here from the future to warn you. In three years from now, you'll be diagnosed with liver cancer and die in agonising pain."

She laughed brazenly, right in my face.

"Is that the best you can do?"

She turned towards the kitchen cupboard, opened up the door, grabbed a wine glass, and then reached for an unopened bottle of red wine in the criss-cross-shaped wine rack that sat on the kitchen surface next to the kettle.

"Well, if I've only got three years left, I'd better get started then, hadn't I?" she remarked, reaching for the screw top of the bottle.

"Mum, please, listen…" I began, attempting to reason with her.

"Listen to your imaginary stories?" She laughed. "Grow, up Amy. You're twenty-two, not two."

She wrenched the cap from the bottle and filled the glass almost to the brim. Then she defiantly took a huge swig, right in front of my face.

I turned away, unable to stomach seeing any more. This hadn't worked. I was doing no good here whatsoever. I still had a plan B, which was to give her Wednesday's lottery numbers as proof I knew the future, but would that make any difference? My sister's death had set her on a course of self-destruction, and she was already past the point of no return.

Abandoning my lottery plan, it was clear that there was only one course of action left open to me now.

I had to save Rachel.

Chapter Fifteen
2004

It was New Year's Eve, 2004, and I was in the living hell-hole that was Phuket, Thailand. It was five days after the catastrophic tsunami that had claimed so many thousands of lives, including my sister's.

I had been steeling myself for this moment for the past few days, knowing where I would find myself. Even so, coming back here after so long still brought it all back home to me. From the moment I arrived, I was filled with emotions as raw as I had felt the first time around, twenty years ago.

I had tried to enjoy my previous two trips but the knowledge of what was to come had weighed heavily upon my mind.

On the day before I turned twenty-one, Kelly and I travelled down to London to see Kylie Minogue in her Showgirl concert. I had been looking forward to this ever since I found the faded ticket in my biscuit tin, and it didn't disappoint on any level.

I had been a fan of Kylie's ever since I was tiny. I couldn't remember her being in *Neighbours*, though I knew she had been because Rachel had told me all about it.

When Kylie rose out of the stage dressed in her pink Showgirl outfit and began belting out *Better the Devil You Know*, the whole crowd, me included, went crazy. This had been one of my early favourite songs, coming out as it did when I was about four years old. She couldn't have picked a better song to open with, and the night just got better and better from there.

In 2005, nothing notable happened around New Year, which was hardly surprising considering I had lost my sister and my father in the space of just over a year. So this time I decided to take the opportunity to go travelling again to see in 2006, realising that it would be just about my last chance. My adulthood was coming to an end.

As I regressed into my teens, my financial muscle was becoming seriously diminished. I got my first credit card as a student at the age of nineteen, so this would be the last year I would be able to make use of it. The limit on it wasn't great, just £1000, but it was enough to get me down to the Canary Islands for one last mini-holiday as I prepared for my arrival in Thailand.

As I lay by the pool on my twentieth birthday there was no escaping the truth that my time was running out. I was now halfway through this journey, and I was going to have a lot less control over what happened to me in the second half.

Soon I would have no money. I would officially be a minor, under the care of parents and teachers. Sure, in my teens it wouldn't be too bad, but what happened when I got even younger? I would have less and less freedom with each passing year.

I also worried about what was going to happen to my body and my mind. The physical changes were inevitable, but how would my mind react? Would my thoughts still be those of an adult, or would I revert to a childlike state, almost like becoming senile in reverse?

All of that was still to come, but for now, I had to put it to the back of my mind and focus on the task at hand, which was the very pressing need to do something about Rachel.

Unlike many of my recent trips from so far back in the past, I was confident about exactly where I was going to find myself when I materialised in Phuket on the morning of 31st December 2004. As my mind took possession of my body from twenty years ago, I realised I was right. I was exactly where I had expected to be. It was where I had spent every day in the immediate aftermath of the disaster.

I was down on the beach, in front of the café where I had been taking breakfast on the morning the tsunami had struck. I had been in Thailand visiting my sister and it was the first time I had travelled abroad alone, aged just eighteen.

Rachel had spent six months travelling the world since graduating the previous summer and had invited me to come out and spend some time with her. I had been very fortunate to be able to get a cheap flight over to spend two weeks with her over Christmas and New Year. My parents weren't particularly keen on me travelling all that way alone at such a tender age, but both Rachel and I had reassured them that it would all be fine. How wrong we had been.

When I said I was in front of the café, I should have said I was in front of where the café used to be. It simply wasn't there anymore. The outer shell of the building that had housed it was still there, but anything that wasn't bolted down had been swept away by the giant waves that had crashed in that day, sucking everything back down to the beach with them as they retreated.

The umbrellas, tables, chairs and various other bits of debris from that café were now scattered all around me, along with numerous other items from the buildings and streets, even whole cars and trucks. Nothing that had been in the firing line of one of nature's most devastating forces was safe. The beach and everything for some considerable distance inland now resembled an overflowing landfill site.

The clean-up operation had barely begun yet. The disaster had only happened five days ago and the search was still continuing for survivors. That was exactly why I was still here. Most of the Brits that had been here had been evacuated but I had refused to leave, desperate to find Rachel.

By this stage, I had known that there was probably little hope. Very few survivors had been found after the first twenty-four hours, so arriving here again on New Year's Eve was of little use to me now. If only I had some element of control over my time travel. If I could have timed my arrival here a week earlier I could have saved her.

What could I have done differently? I thought back over the events of that morning. There were plenty of things I could have done. The tsunami had not come in until late morning. I could have found her and got her to higher ground. I could also have saved more than just her – hundreds, if not thousands, of people. That's assuming I could convince people to heed my warnings.

How was it that I had survived and Rachel hadn't? It was largely down to my excessive drinking whilst celebrating Christmas the previous evening.

Both of us had been at a party on the beach with many others that had gone on very late, but Rachel had gone to bed considerably earlier than me. Had I not stayed out, I would very likely have been on the beach at the time the tsunami struck leading to me joining Rachel in her watery grave.

She had left much earlier than me, having met a charming Frenchman and accepting his invite to go back to his hotel with him. My sister was only three years older than me, but that made a huge difference at that time when it came to our sex lives. At twenty-one, with three years at university behind her, she was confident sexually. In contrast, I was still finding my feet, having had just one boyfriend.

She winked at me as she left that night, handing me her room key and telling me not to wait up. It was the last time I ever saw her.

The following morning, I had come down late. Not only was I sexually inexperienced at eighteen, but I was also still finding my way with alcohol. I hadn't yet learnt when to stop and had stayed out far later than I should have.

I had eventually gone back to the hotel so much the worse for wear with drink that I was unable to surface until late morning. When I did, I had just about managed to make my way down to the café and order some breakfast, hiding behind dark glasses, when I became aware that something wasn't right.

The veranda of the café overlooked the already busy beach. It made for a pretty scene, fringed with palm trees beyond which were scattered rocks on the white sands. But this morning there was something different about the view.

I couldn't see the shoreline, the water having retreated far further than I had ever seen it. What I could see were people on the beach wandering far out onto the exposed seabed, presumably curious as to the cause of this strange phenomenon. They didn't seem to have any inkling that there might be any danger, but I felt a sudden premonition about what was about to happen.

A memory stirred in me about a children's book I had read many years earlier about a young woman trapped on a desert island. In the story, I remember something similar occurring, and what followed it was something terrifying. It was something that I had heard referred to wrongly in the past as a tidal wave, but I knew it by the correct name – a tsunami.

Instinctively, I knew these foolhardy people wandering far out onto a seabed that had never been exposed before. My first thought had been to jump up and shout a warning, but they were a good half a mile away, some of them. Besides, looking further out to the horizon, I quickly realised I was too late.

Some of the people furthest out had turned back and were running back up the beach but they were already doomed. There was no way they would be able to outrun the huge surge of water racing up behind them and I watched horrified as it began to swallow them up.

It wasn't a huge, towering wave as I had seen tsunamis portrayed in Hollywood movies. It was more a huge surge of water, relentlessly sweeping all before it in its path and it was coming towards me fast.

I couldn't save the people on the beach but I jumped up and yelled at everyone in the café, all of whom still seemed oblivious to what was going on.

"Tsunami! Run for your lives!"

I was expecting everyone to start screaming, but they didn't, just looking at me as if I was crazy. I wasn't waiting around to try and convince them, I needed to follow my own advice. Sidestepping the waiter, who unbelievably tried to block my way, thinking I was trying to get out of paying the bill, I ran out of the café and as fast as I could up the street away from the beach.

Even with the head start I had on all the other people who were only now starting to twig what was happening, I could hear the water rushing up behind me. I can still remember now, twenty years later, the sheer panic I felt when I realised I wasn't going to be able to outrun it.

Thankfully for me, as I passed the low balcony of a hotel on my right, I was spotted by two British middle-aged men, in Union Jack shorts with pot bellies.

"Up here, love!" one of them called over the sound of the onrushing water.

There was a car parked just below their window so I scrambled aboard, and they pulled me up, just as the water reached the car.

Then it began to subside. Perhaps this wasn't going to be as bad as I feared after all. Grateful to my two hosts for the rescue, I eagerly took the beer that they offered. Despite my raging hangover, I was seriously in need of a drink.

We watched in horrified fascination as the water retreated, sucking back bottles, plastic furniture and all manner of other stuff with it before the shocking realisation hit us that it wasn't all over. It was going to be much worse than I had initially feared.

A second, much bigger wave crashed in, this time passing our position and sweeping the car I had climbed upon up the road as if it was a boat. All around people were screaming and I saw more than one disappear beneath the water, having been knocked over by cars, bins and other heavy objects.

The water was everywhere and sweeping up everything in its path as it pushed on up the street. If I had still been down there, I have no doubt that I would have been killed.

I still feared for my safety, even from the relative safety of the hotel. The water had almost come up the floor of the balcony and would clearly have flooded the ground floor. Would the building be strong enough to hold?

Fortunately, it was a modern hotel block made of concrete that held firm. The same certainly couldn't be said for some of the more lightweight dwellings closer to the shore. For anyone still down there, the outlook would be bleak indeed.

Temporarily safe, my thoughts turned to Rachel. Was she safe? I didn't even know where she had spent the night. All I knew was she had left with the Frenchman and I couldn't even recall his name. It might possibly have been Pierre, but that was barely more than a guess. Addled with alcohol as I had been, small details such as the names of people I had met at the party had simply not stuck.

I recalled the happy, smiley faces of the previous evening, dancing around the fire in what was then paradise on earth.

How many of them were still alive now in what had become the complete opposite?

As the water retreated a second time, the true cost of the disaster was becoming apparent. One of my companions was recording everything on a handheld camcorder and it made for grim viewing. Everything was being dragged back down the street by the retreating flood water, not just all the jetsam and flotsam that had been generated by the wave, but people, too.

Some were still screaming for help, but others were motionless apart from the contortions the water was wreaking on their bodies as it twisted them to and fro like rag dolls.

When the lifeless body of a girl, no more than five or six years old floated past, I had to turn away from the balcony and dash into the bathroom where I was physically and horribly sick.

This wasn't just the throwing up of someone who'd had too much to drink the night before. I was sick with shock, panic and fear. I was only eighteen – I was too young to be coping with this alone, but there was no big sister beside me to lean on. The fear I felt for my own safety began to be replaced by fear for her. I prayed that she was still shacked up in bed with the Frenchman, safely out of harm's way. I didn't dare even contemplate the possibility that she might have been down on the beach.

I had my mobile phone with me and tried calling her number but I couldn't get any sort of signal. It seemed all communications were out. As soon as the waters subsided again, I thanked the two men who had helped me, and dashed back out into the street, despite them warning me it might be too dangerous.

It was a scene of sheer carnage. Desperately I ran, calling her name, as I skirted around everything from upturned cars to fridge freezers which were scattered everywhere. I wasn't alone by any means. There were dozens out there in a similarly distressed state going through exactly what I was – locals and tourists alike.

Invariably I came across more bodies and forced myself to look at the faces of at least three girls who could have been Rachel. When I saw that they weren't I felt a strange mix of emotions. There was relief at the discovery that they weren't Rachel, tempered with an increasing desperation at not finding her.

I also felt more than a tinge of guilt at feeling relief as the friends and relatives of these poor souls were ultimately going to suffer the grief of discovering their lifeless bodies.

It seemed like I had been stumbling around for hours when the first relief teams began to arrive. It took a long time for them to get there. This wasn't just a case of ambulances and fire engines rolling up at an incident because the incident was widespread. They were needed everywhere.

This had all happened five days before I arrived back here on my latest trip through time. The relief effort had spent most of those five days recovering, removing and identifying bodies. Most surviving tourists had been evacuated. I had still been here because I had refused to leave with the other evacuees, I had spent those days scouring the shoreline for miles in both directions, desperately searching for any sign of Rachel.

I asked around the hotels, desperate to track down where the Frenchman had been staying, but it was no good. I had nothing to go on other than a vague stab at a first name. There was nothing else, not even a photo. Had this been a few years later when I and everyone else was snapping everything that moved and plastering it all over social media, I might have stood a chance, but people didn't do that yet in 2004.

I knew now, arriving on 31st December, that continuing to search for Rachel would be pointless. I hadn't found her before and I wouldn't find her now. Her body had never been found, presumably swallowed up by the sea like so many others. There was only one thing I could do right now – the same thing that I had ultimately done before, several days later.

I abandoned my search for my sister and joined the relief effort. The other aid workers were only too grateful for my help. Joining in with them before had given me a sense of purpose, and it was this that had inspired me to begin working with the Red Cross in the years that followed.

As for Rachel, I had to stop her from coming here. It was as simple as that. But would it be that easy? I remembered my attempts to stop my mother's drinking. She had rubbished my claims of time-travelling from the future, and who wouldn't? Rachel might well do the same.

It's not as if I could even provide her with any proof that the tsunami was going to happen. If I could take a picture of this beach right here and take it back through time with me, I would. But that wasn't possible.

I couldn't prove the tsunami was going to happen, but I didn't need to. When I next went back a year in time I would have only two days to convince Rachel. I had already done my homework and intended to pump her with so much irrefutable proof that I could tell the future that she would ensure she was nowhere near the Indian Ocean on Boxing Day.

I looked around me once more at the devastation.

No Rachel – there is no way you are dying here.

Chapter Sixteen
2003

The trouble with trying to remember things that took place over twenty years ago was that I could remember major events, such as the party to celebrate my coming of age stuck in my mind, but not the details around them. The human brain, mine anyway, had only so much storage capacity on the hard drive and selectively sent anything not considered important to the recycle bin.

This made planning ahead difficult, particularly when I had such an important task in front of me. Fortunately, the time I had previously spent on the laptop researching past years was about to come in very handy.

My bedroom had changed noticeably since the last time I had arrived in it. The rocky bands I had been into in the mid-noughties were no longer in evidence, and the walls were now decorated with posters of the Spice Girls.

Had I really still had those up approaching my eighteenth birthday? Even in 2003, which seems like a lifetime ago now, they were seriously old hat. The group had long disbanded by this time and most of the girls were enjoying solo careers.

I had been woken up by my digital clock radio alarm going off, which was tuned into Fox FM, the local radio station at the time. It was playing, appropriately enough, one of the Spice Girls' solo songs, "Free Me" by Emma Bunton. She had always been my favourite Spice Girl and was having a string of hits around this time.

The song finished and was replaced by "Mad World", which I recalled had been Christmas Number One that year. The list of festive chart-toppers had been one of the things I had memorised during my internet research.

I lay in bed for a while, wondering where all the years had gone. 2003 didn't seem like more than twenty years ago. It felt like a decade at the most. Had I wasted my life, letting the years fly the way they had?

It was the same for everyone, I guess. No one can fight against the inevitable passing of time. That's what I used to think, anyway. Now my perspective was somewhat different.

My musing was interrupted by my mother calling me from downstairs.

"Are you coming down, Amy? You're going to be late for work."

I was temporarily flummoxed by this. Where was work? That was something I had neglected to check up on. I thought for a moment then remembered that, over that Christmas and New Year, I had been working in a café in town, waiting tables.

This was one of many different jobs I had held as a teenager, trying to save as much money as I could so I could emulate my sister and go travelling in the future. It was largely money earned during 2004 working everywhere from Burger King to B&Q that had enabled me to join Rachel in Thailand that ill-fated Christmas.

Was I going to work today? I had ducked out sick so many times from the hospital during my time travels that a shift serving coffee and sandwiches in the Covered Market wasn't any big deal. However, I had really enjoyed that job and saw no reason not to go. It would all be rather nostalgic, like much of my life.

My home couldn't have looked more different to how it had during my mother's declining years. As I descended the stairs towards the kitchen I could see that everything looked spotless. There wasn't a hint of fluff on the fawn-coloured

189

carpet that covered the stairs, nor was there a speck of dust in the hallway.

The kitchen, likewise, was immaculate, surfaces sparkling clean, a vase of freshly cut flowers in the centre of the table and the smell of home-cooked bread filling the air. My mother was smart and carried the poise of a happy and confident woman as she turned at hearing my approach, handing me a freshly brewed cup of coffee.

"Here, you'd better get that down you," she said.

Happy as I was to see my mother back to her old self before the tsunami shattered her world, it wasn't her I needed to see.

"Where's Rachel?" I asked.

"Down in London," replied Mum. "I thought you knew. She won't be back until after New Year."

This was a bad start.

"Where in London?" I asked.

"You're not thinking of trying to go down to join her, by any chance, are you? We already discussed this, remember?"

Now she mentioned it, I did remember. I had wanted to go and see in the New Year in London with Rachel but my mother had insisted on me staying at home, saying I could go next year when I was eighteen. This was the problem with being the younger sibling. It always seemed that the older one got to have all the fun.

Saying I could go when I was eighteen felt rather harsh at the time, seeing as I was just one day short of that milestone but I had reluctantly agreed with my mother promising to arrange a party to celebrate my birthday.

My first thought now was that I could tell Rachel at the party. It could wait another day, but then I noticed a return slip from a party invite pinned to the fridge by a magnet from Tenby. It clearly stated the date of the party as Saturday 3rd January 2004.

Of course, I remembered now. It had been decided not to have the party on New Year's Day for the same reason that I had been coming up against all my life. No one wanted to party on 1st January with their hangovers from the night before. Rachel had definitely been at the party: she had been back from London by then, but that was no good to me now as I would be gone by then.

This was frustrating. Why was nothing ever simple? There was nothing else for it: I was going to have to defy my mother and go to London. I wasn't enjoying, as someone used to adult independence, that I could or couldn't do something, and it was only going to get worse. What would it be like when I was six or seven and I was being told to eat my greens and to go to bed at half past seven?

Thankfully, at seventeen I still had enough power to make my own decisions. I just hoped I could get enough money together to get myself down to London.

Getting to London was only half the battle: I still had to find Rachel when I got there. Fortunately, I still had a mobile phone, even if it was only a basic Nokia. I could text her.

I had no idea who she was with or what she was doing: those details were lost in the mists of time. Whoever it was, I can't imagine she was going to be particularly enamoured with her little sister gatecrashing the party, but tough – her life depended on it. She would thank me one day, even if I wasn't going to be around to hear it.

I went upstairs, pretending to get ready for work, and texted Rachel. If I was expecting an immediate response, I was to be disappointed. Wherever she was, she was probably still asleep. It was only just after 8am after all.

191

Opening my wardrobe, I found an impossibly small uniform from the café that I couldn't believe I could possibly fit into, but it slid on easily with room to spare. I was getting smaller and slimmer by the year, and my slender frame was barely that of a woman now.

I may have had no intention of going to work, but I wanted my mother to think everything was normal. I didn't want to have to get into a round of explanations with her, not after my previous attempts.

Everything went smoothly until after I left the house and reached the cashpoint. Then I realised I had a problem. Thumbing through yet another new wallet, I discovered that my bank card had changed. No longer was I with HSBC. My card was now from Barclays. Worse still, when I tried to put my PIN in, it wouldn't accept it.

Once again, long-forgotten memories came flooding back. I had changed my bank account in my late teens after running into some overdraft problems as a student and parting company with Barclays on acrimonious terms. Now I was back with them, I couldn't for the life of me remember my PIN.

Frantically I searched through my wallet and purse in which I kept my loose coins. I had a total of £3.57 on me and that wasn't going to get me to London, not even at 2003 prices. I was going to have to get some money from somewhere else.

Desperate times called for desperate measures. I didn't feel good about what I was about to do, but I had done worse things. This was hardly on the same scale as causing Gary's death, and besides, it was going to save a life, not end one. That was all the justification I needed.

I took the short walk back to the house. My mother was surprised to see me, but I explained I had forgotten my purse and pretended to go upstairs. While she busied herself in the kitchen, I helped myself to fifty quid out of her wallet which was in her handbag, conveniently hanging on the hatstand close to the front door.

"Sorry, Mum," I murmured to myself, "but it's all for a good cause."

As long as I kept telling myself that, it would all be good. I had never stolen off my parents in my life – or anyone, come to that. This was most definitely a one-off.

Funding in place, I headed straight for the train station. Twice more I tried to ring Rachel on the way, and both times it went straight to voicemail. What was she doing? She had better have her phone on her as there was no way I was going to be able to track her down otherwise. I would just have to text her again.

Rachel, why aren't you answering your phone? I need to speak to you urgently.

That ought to do it. It was sufficiently vague to hopefully worry her or at least pique her curiosity enough to contact me. That's assuming she ever got around to looking at her phone.

At the train station, I popped into WHSmith and bought a notebook and a pen. I had left in such a hurry that I hadn't had time to put into place a vital part of my plan.

Thankfully, the train was not too busy so I was able to find a place with a seat, even if it wasn't the most appetising spot. Someone had left an apple core on the seat and there were crumbs all over the table but it would have to do. As soon as the train was in motion, I pulled my purchases out of my bag and began to write.

By the time the train pulled into Paddington, I had emptied every scrap of information I could remember about 2004 into the notebook. That time spent at the laptop learning all this had been time well spent. But none of it was going to be any good unless Rachel rang.

I had left my mobile on the table in front of me for the whole journey, but still no joy. What was worse, my battery was down to 13% and I had no charger. From what I remembered, these old Nokias were pretty decent on battery life but even so, 13% was not going to last long.

I had filled about five pages of the notebook, and I cast my eye now over the first page, wondering if what I had written would be enough. It was heavily biased towards the start of the year because I had concentrated on January for a reason. I had figured that if I ever needed to convince anybody of my knowledge of the future, the sooner the events took place, the better.

There's going to be a plane crash near Egypt on 3rd January which will kill all 148 people aboard.

Harold Shipman is going to hang himself in prison on 13th January.

Janet Jackson is going to have a wardrobe malfunction at the Super Bowl on 1st February.

Manchester United are going to beat Millwall 3-0 in the FA Cup final.

And so it went on, for another four pages. It ended with a detailed description of the Boxing Day tsunami. If this didn't convince Rachel, nothing would, but I still had to get it to her.

Just as I was getting off the train, my phone rang. It was her. The timing wasn't great, as it was very busy and noisy in the station, but I just about managed to make out what she was saying.

"What's up, little sis?" she said.

I could barely answer as I had become quite choked with emotion at hearing her voice for the first time in over twenty years. My sister was alive! Now that I had heard her speak, suddenly it was all real.

"I'll explain when I see you," I replied, trying to sound as normal as possible. "I'm in London. Where are you?"

She was rather taken aback to hear where I was and didn't sound too pleased. Rather than try and explain over the phone with the noise of engines and platform announcements all around me, I got her to agree to meet me in half an hour beneath Nelson's Column.

She was alone when I met her and looking none too happy.

"What's all this about, Amy?" she demanded. "I had to cut short lunch with friends to come and meet you."

Her grumpy demeanour couldn't dampen my mood. I was just overwhelmingly happy to see my long-dead sister in the flesh once more. I ran up to her and almost knocked her over as I flung myself at her slender frame, burying my head in her long, wavy, dark hair that was just tinted with a hint of red.

"Whoa! Steady on, sis," she replied, pushing me away and seeing the tears in my eyes that had welled up the moment I had grabbed hold of her. I looked back into her piercing, green eyes, a mirror image of my own, and for a moment, couldn't think of anything to say.

"Are you in some kind of trouble?" she asked. "Mum rang me while I was waiting for you. She says some money's gone missing from her purse."

"Does she think I took it?" I asked.

"She wanted to know where you were, but she never suggested that it was you. I doubt the possibility had even occurred to her that you would do such a thing. It wasn't you, was it?"

"It was me, Rachel," I confessed.

"Oh Amy, how could you?" she replied, a look of disappointment in her eyes. "Stealing from our own mother? Why?"

195

"Rachel, it was an emergency, quite literally a matter of life and death. I had to take the money so I could get down here to see you. I had to warn you that your life is in danger."

That was possibly a little overdramatic as a look of fear flashed across her face.

"What is it, Amy? Does somebody want to hurt me?"

I had to be careful how I worded this.

"God, no," I replied. "It's nothing like that, but you have to listen to me – please. Forget what you are meant to be doing today, this is far more important. Let's go and grab some lunch and I'll explain it all."

She looked back at me with those lovely green eyes, so full of life, and now displaying more than a degree of curiosity. There was no way I was letting that life be snuffed out.

"Alright, Amy, you've got an hour, and this had better not be a wind-up."

We went into one of the many branches of Garfunkel's in the West End, ordered burgers and shakes, and I began the long process of explaining about the tsunami, and her involvement in it. Sceptical at first, she began to come around when I presented her with the notebook, but I knew it was going to take time for her to fully believe because none of these events had happened yet.

"Just keep that notebook and don't lose it," I urged her. "When that plane crashes in three days, you will know I am telling the truth and if that doesn't convince you, there is plenty more that will. Above all, you have to promise me you won't go to Thailand this Christmas."

"OK, I won't," she said, still not fully convinced, "as long as the rest of this stuff comes true. But there's one thing you haven't explained about all of this. How did you come by all of this knowledge in the first place?"

196

I realised I was going to have to tell her the whole story, something I hadn't done with anyone up until now. I had tried to tell my mother some of it in my attempt to stop her drinking, but she had cut me off before I had been able to explain properly. Other than my seemingly futile letter to Professor Hamilton, that was all I had told anyone.

Having kept all of this to myself for so long it was a huge relief to finally be able to unburden myself to Rachel.

"If all of this is true, Amy, then you will have to warn me about all of this again next year. And the year after that – or do I mean the year before that? You will have to tell me every year, otherwise, how will I know if you keep going back to a time before you have told me?"

"I'm not sure it works like that," I said. "I've been trying to figure out how my actions in the past affect the future. One theory is that I am creating multiple futures."

"So in some possible future, I'm still dead?" she asked.

"Yes, but the important thing is, you're alive in this one and now you know how to stay alive."

"And that won't all be undone when you go back another year in time?" she asked.

"I just have no way of really knowing," I replied, recognising her line of reasoning because they were the same thought processes I had been through hundreds of times.

"All I can do is try and do my best for the future any way I can," I added.

"And what about Mum?" asked Rachel. "Are you going to explain all of this to her? What about the money you stole from her? How are you going to justify that?"

"Well, I was planning on jumping back into the past before that became an issue," I replied. "Escaping into the past has got me out of quite a few scrapes."

"Such as?" she asked.

"Oh, nothing particularly exciting," I replied.

I had no intention of telling her about the sordid activities that had led to Gary's death. She didn't need to know all of that. She didn't even know who Gary was and it was years in a future that probably wouldn't happen that way – not in this world at least.

"But what about you, Amy?" she asked. "You came here to save me, but what about your predicament? What's going to happen to you?"

"I'm pretty much resigned to my fate, Rach. I'm just going to keep going back in time, getting younger and younger until a time before I was born. Then I will simply cease to exist."

"But the body you are in now? That will stay?"

"That's what I think will happen. I will still be here, with you, presumably the same as I was before my mind jumped into this body. You won't lose me."

"But the version of you that's in there, now. The one I'm talking to right now. You'll vanish, so will the original you remember any of this?"

"I've no idea. I've never been around to find out. All I know is that this version of me, this soul that inhabits this body right now, is doomed. I know that and I've already accepted my fate."

There had been tears in my eyes when I had found Rachel again. Now it was my sister's turn to cry.

Chapter Seventeen
1999

The world was preparing to usher in a new millennium, one that I had already seen the first quarter century of. Now here I was, at the age of thirteen being allowed my official first glass of champagne – which sadly would also be my last.

Firsts and lasts were becoming a regular feature of my life these days. On New Year's Day 2003 I had simultaneously lost my virginity and had sex for the final time in my life, two events which ought to have been separated by several decades.

It had been with Max who had popped my cherry. He was my teenage boyfriend and first love whom I had been with between the ages of sixteen and eighteen. I had missed him the previous year when I had gone down to see Rachel in London, so 2003 had been my only opportunity to see him. I was determined to make the most of it.

The first time around we had been a couple for many months before we lost our virginity together in the Easter holidays, but given the circumstances, I was determined to bring that forward.

It wasn't difficult to accomplish. He had spent most of the autumn crafting the most beautifully articulate love letters to me and we had spent much time passionately kissing, with me firmly removing his wandering hands when they strayed close to my nether regions.

I considered myself to be a good girl and wanted to wait until I was ready. I certainly wasn't going to rush into anything like some of the girls in my class, two of whom were already pregnant. I was going to be properly prepared, and my sister had helped in this by kindly supplying me with condoms, advising me that men had a tendency to forget if they could get away with it.

I had a lovely night with Max, though the action was all over rather quickly the first time. In his extreme excitement at finally achieving the Holy Grail of every heterosexual teenage male on the planet, Max's initial adventure into my nether regions lasted somewhere around thirty seconds.

On the plus side, he had an amazing recovery window, and since I had cunningly convinced my mother I was staying at Kelly's for the night, I had the whole night with Max as he had successfully managed to smuggle me into his room without his drunk parents noticing. Over the next six or seven hours, we managed to do it four times, and thankfully he had slowed down considerably for the later rounds.

Before I left 2003 behind me, I made sure I briefed Rachel again about avoiding Thailand, something she had suggested. I would need to carry on doing this every year as long as I could.

After 2003, things began to get rather dull. Just as I had anticipated, my freedom continued to decline as I worked my way back through my teenage years.

Schooldays are supposedly the best days of your life, but they weren't in my case, at least not in my early teenage years. After I had moved down from Merseyside in the late-1990s to a new school in Oxford, I had been the constant target of ribbing about my accent. Brookside was still on TV at the time, along with Harry Enfield and his Scousers sketch.

As soon as the other kids at school realised I was from Liverpool I was subject to a constant barrage of "calm down, calm down". I also had to put up with constant jibes about not leaving anything lying about because I might nick it. I had never stolen anything in my life – unless you count the money I had taken from my mother's bag, but that was a) an emergency, and b) in the future.

Over time, the locals became more accepting of me. I made friends and even began to enjoy school. I wasn't going to be able to revisit any of those carefree and responsibility-free times on this journey, though. My timing, being stuck in New Year for all eternity, was lousy. It was smack bang in the middle of the school holidays.

On a positive note, my birthday began to assume a greater level of importance. It seemed the younger I became, the more fuss was made. Some years, this involved family gatherings, which each time brought back long-gone family members into my life, as grandparents, uncles and aunts came back to life and made their reappearances.

Some years brought days out with friends, including a very memorable fifteenth birthday outing in 2001, when Mum, Rachel, Kelly and I got to go and see the recently opened musical, *The Lion King*, in London. This had been one of my favourite movies as a kid and I remember begging my mother to take us to the stage show.

The tickets hadn't been cheap and she had to book them nearly a year in advance, but it had been well worth it. Getting to see this amazing show a second time around was a real highlight of my trip back through time.

And now it was the end of the Millennium – a significant milepost in the life of pretty much everyone alive at that time. The human race was saying goodbye to a century that had brought amazing technological developments from the aeroplane to the internet that had completely changed the world. Now, they were putting all of that behind them and wondering what this brave new dawn would bring.

I was in the unique position of having already seen it. Most were looking to the new century with optimism, but was it misplaced? I knew that, despite further advances, the first quarter of a century would bring difficult times: more wars, more pollution and great political upheaval.

Above all else, the world would change forever on September 11th 2001 with the terror attacks in America. But the world was blissfully unaware of this now, and as I looked at the faces all around me, I saw something I saw every New Year – hope.

Hope was something of which I was in short supply. But tonight, I resolved that I must put all that behind me and make the most to enjoy the evening.

I was at my grandparents' house in Botley, where they had invited family and friends from far and wide to celebrate this special year. There were about forty people there all told, spread out around the kitchen, living room and conservatory.

The evening had been a source of delight for me. It had given me the chance to catch up with many long-lost family members. My Uncle Derek and his family had come down from Banbury to join us. He had two daughters, Kirsty and Karen, who were a little older than me and Rachel. They had got into drinking and boys before we did, and we both looked up to them. They were also very handy for smuggling drink in our direction at these sorts of gatherings.

Uncle Derek had proved to be tremendous entertainment value throughout the evening, with his ongoing attempts to convince everyone that the Millennium bug was about to strike, bringing the world to an end.

Despite being only in his mid-forties, Derek was quite an old-fashioned man, as amply demonstrated by both his attire, an old-fashioned beige suit, and his attitudes. These included not only a deep suspicion of anything foreign but also a mistrust of any new technology.

"I'm telling you," I heard him saying to my mother, "people might take the piss, but they won't be laughing when planes start dropping out of the sky at midnight. I've been preparing for this for weeks."

"Don't I know it?" chipped in his wife, my Aunty Carol. "I'm sick of tripping over the boxes of candles all over the house."

I liked my Aunty Carol. She was in her late forties around this time and wore way too much perfume and make-up to cover up her years. I remembered the constant banter she and her husband used to have whenever I encountered them in my youth.

"You may scoff, my dear," replied Derek, taking a puff on his old-fashioned pipe and holding it out in front of him as if that somehow gave him an air of wisdom and authority. "But you'll be glad of those candles tomorrow night – and the Calor Gas stove."

"Yes, and I'm sick of that bloody thing cluttering up the hallway too," replied Carol.

"Covered every base, I have," continued Derek, ignoring his wife's remark. "That Brian next door, he thinks I'm a nutter, but I'm going to be the one laughing tomorrow night when he's freezing cold and begging to come in and get warm in front of my wood burner."

"Ooh, you've got a wood burner, now?" asked my mother.

"Yes, and that's set us back a fair few bob, as well," complained Carol. "It's dirty, smelly and messy. Then there are all the logs we have to lug into the house. I swear they've got things living in them. When I came down this morning, there were silverfish running around on the kitchen floor and we've never had them before."

"You can't beat a real fire, though," replied my mother.

"Don't encourage him," said Carol. "Tomorrow morning, when all this is over, all that stuff he's piled up everywhere is going straight back in the garage. And if he insists on using that wood burner, he can clean it out himself."

"If you say, so dear," replied Derek condescendingly.

"If it's going to bad as you say, how come you are here now?" asked my mother. "Shouldn't you be at home, preparing for the worst?"

"Well, I was invited and I couldn't let the family down, could I?" he replied.

"More like you didn't want to miss out on all the free food and booze on offer," retorted his wife.

"What's that awful racket?" complained Derek, deciding wisely to change the subject. The music, which had already been distinctly modern for the generally conservative gathering in the room, had suddenly been ratcheted up a notch.

I grinned as the dulcet tones of Eminem rudely drowned out the conversation. Kirsty's boyfriend, Mark, who claimed to be a part-time DJ, had unwisely been allowed to bring his decks along for the evening. That is if you could call them that.

His equipment consisted of a cheap twin-CD bedroom starter kit from Argos, which he had plugged into my grandfather's old-fashioned Pioneer stereo system. Apparently, Mark had planned to bring his speakers but had discovered at the last minute that there wasn't enough room for them in the boot of Uncle Derek's fifteen-year-old Mini Metro.

Despite the basic nature of the set-up, it was surprisingly loud in the relatively small living room. This hadn't been a problem, to begin with, but as the evening wore on, I watched with amusement as the music deviated more and more away from the brief. Mark had been under strict instructions to play

20th-century music from across the eras suitable for all age groups.

He had interpreted this as playing a few tunes from the 60s and 70s at the start of the night to keep the old folk happy, followed more or less exclusively by music he liked. As a young man in his early twenties, this pretty much meant tunes from the 1990s. While Rachel, Kirsty, Karen and I loved this, needless to say, the older generation did not.

I remembered all this with glee from the first time around and now chuckled as my uncle's face went as red as a beetroot in outrage at the lyrics to Eminem's "My Name Is", and this wasn't the radio-edit version.

I followed as he marched over to Mark, keen not to miss out on the inevitable confrontation. Unsurprisingly, Derek didn't like his daughter's boyfriend. He was twenty-one and his precious Kirsty was eighteen, which meant that there was a high probability that he was screwing her.

My uncle, who was of the old school 'no sex before marriage' type definitely would not be happy about that.

"What the bloody hell is this?!" spluttered Derek into his beer, a bottle of something called mild, whatever that was. "This is supposed to be a family party. It's half past eleven on New Year's Eve and you're playing this disgusting, filthy stuff. We want some proper good, old-fashioned party tunes."

"Well, I was sort of saving those until after midnight," replied Mark.

"That's no bloody good, is it?" shouted Derek, struggling to compete with Eminem's swearing. "You know all the power's going to go off at midnight when this Millennium bug hits, don't you? Now get this vile rubbish off and play some proper tunes."

205

I was standing right behind and saw an opportunity to intervene.

"Maybe I can help out," I said. "I know my music."

"You," said Mark, scornfully. "How old are you, about ten?"

I bristled at this put-down and replied. "Nearly fourteen, as it happens, and believe me, I can guarantee I've been to a lot more New Year parties than you."

"Yes, let her help," said Rachel who had come up behind me. "If anyone knows about New Year's Eve here, she does."

Earlier that day, I had given Rachel my now standard tsunami warning chat so she knew all about my time travels.

"Come on, lad," said Derek. "You've had your chance and made a pig's ear of it. Move over and let these girls sort it out."

Quickly I flicked through the big box of CDs Mark had brought with him, pulling out a compilation album of party hits.

"Here, try this," I said. "Track Five."

Muttering, Mark took the CD and put it in the spare deck. A few seconds later Eminem's lyrics were cut short as the opening chords to Dexys Midnight Runners' "Come On Eileen" rang out.

"Hmm, that's a bit better," said Derek, begrudgingly, "but still a little modern for my tastes."

"Well, they all seem to like it," said Rachel, gesturing towards the room where a large proportion of the guests, even the grandparents, had spontaneously begun to dance for the first time that evening.

I wasn't a massive fan of this song personally, having heard it done to death over so many New Year parties, but I knew how effective it always was on this particular night.

Over the next half-hour, I produced a set that included, amongst others, "Rock Around The Clock", "Dancing Queen", "Don't You Want Me?" and "The Final Countdown". At five minutes to midnight, I topped the whole thing off with Prince's *1999*. It was cheesy and obvious but nobody cared. I was giving them exactly what they wanted.

The TV was switched on to hear Big Ben's bongs just before midnight arrived. Much to Uncle Derek's disappointment, the lights didn't go off and no planes crashed on the house. That was when I had that official first glass of champagne. Of course, being a teenager it wasn't my first drink of the evening. No one knew about the cider that Kirsty had smuggled upstairs for us kids to share earlier in the evening.

It was a time when alcohol, like so many things, was new, forbidden and therefore exciting. Even though I had loved through another twenty-five years since this evening, I didn't feel jaded in any way. There were even moments during the night when I forgot about my situation for a moment and really did revert to that teenage mindset when the endless possibilities of life were still stretching out before me.

But they weren't in front of me anymore. I was heading in the opposite direction and I now had less than four weeks left.

Chapter Eighteen
1992

I am now almost six years old and time is running out.

Strangely, I no longer fear the death that now seems inevitable. What I fear most of all now is my birth.

Although I've never had children myself, I know from countless conversations that childbirth is the worst pain a woman can experience. But what about the process of actually being born? How does that feel? Is it as painful for the baby as the mother?

The answer is that nobody knows. Not everyone has given birth, but everyone has been born – whether that be the normal way or by Caesarean section. In my case, I know it was the former.

We may all have been through it, but none of us can remember it. Our minds are simply too undeveloped to lay down long-term memories of the event at such a tender age. It's not a topic that comes up in conversation that regularly because it's not something that anyone else has ever had to worry about. But I did, and I was approaching the event with more than a degree of trepidation.

What will it be like to be confined in a womb, in the last few hours before birth? I can't imagine anything more claustrophobic. Will I even be aware by then of what is happening? Will the physical changes happening to me mean that I won't be able to remember who I am by then?

It's certainly a possibility. Even now, the day before my seventh birthday I am struggling to hold onto the person I once was. Although the memories of everything I've been through are still there, I can't help but be affected by the changes in my body.

The way I think, the way I feel and the way I behave are all being influenced by my physical state.

I lost interest in boys as I grew younger, seeing them as dirty, smelly creatures, just as I had when I had been a ten-year-old growing up. There were other changes, too. I no longer had any desire to drink alcohol, and when I sneaked a cup of coffee at the age of nine, I spat out the vile, bitter-tasting liquid in disgust.

I remembered an old quote from the bible that my R.E. teacher once made us all write out twice as a punishment for our unruly behaviour. It began something along these lines:

When I was a child, I spake as a child, I understood as a child, I thought as a child: but when I became a man, I put away childish things.

We must have been about fourteen at the time. I think the message the teacher was trying to get across was that we should stop acting like immature brats and grow up. We didn't take much notice of him at the time because we were too busy having a laugh, but ultimately of course, we did grow up.

Now I was going through the process in reverse. Much as I might try to hold onto my adulthood, I could not fight nature, despite the memories of the grown-up I had once been. The environment around me was also becoming more that of a child and with every passing year, more toys and games from the past reappeared in my bedroom. Far from dismissing these toys as childish relics, I seized upon them with delight.

When I became a man, I put away childish things.

OK, I was a woman, not a man, but gender aside, I was now living this quote in reverse. I was getting my childish things out again and loving every minute of it.

Things changed the most dramatically at the age of eleven. That was the first year I found myself back in Liverpool, in our old house in West Derby where I had spent my formative years. In the space of one year, my living space changed dramatically.

No longer did I find myself in the room of a teenager. Gone were the pop posters from the walls, replaced by wallpaper from my adored film, *The Lion King*.

The room was full of new/old toys, and I had seized upon the Tamagotchi I found next to my bed with delight, playing with it for the whole of that day. This was all the proof I needed that I was regressing to a childlike state. It simply wasn't something that would have held any interest for me had I discovered it as an adult, other than a few seconds of curiosity about this ancient toy.

My parents had bought this for me after the death of my beloved cat, to help ease the pain. I had wanted another cat, but they had said it was too dangerous because of the road we lived on.

The room was littered with other toys, from Barbie to Sylvanian Families, all of which I found myself increasingly drawn to as the years passed.

I went back another year in time and my cat reappeared. He was a beautiful ginger and white tabby we had got from a rescue centre when I was just seven years old. I had doted on him and insisted on naming him after a character from *The Lion King* which I had just seen for the first time.

I was heartbroken when he met a sticky end under the wheels of a souped-up Vauxhall Nova. We lived on Coachmans Drive, close to where they used to film the old Brookside series. There was a big problem with boy racers on our road at that time, and I am sure it was one of them who killed him.

There was nothing I could do to prevent my pet's fate. No tsunami-style warning was going to mean anything to a cat. Trying not to think about it, I just got on with enjoying the short time I had with him while I could.

My best friend from primary school, Siobhan, came around that birthday, keen to play with my extensive collection of Sylvanian Families toys, including a lot of new stuff I got given for my birthday that year.

I had no objection to this, again finding myself warming to these childhood activities. It was simple, easy fun, and uncomplicated with the worries of adulthood. I was starting to approach the world with a renewed childlike wonder in my eyes. Memories of the person I had once been were becoming hazy. Was this similar to the experience of old people who got Alzheimer's?

Every year I jumped back now, things seemed to change more and more compared to the year before. The world was getting bigger as I got smaller. By the age of eight, my parents had become giants, my bed seemed enormous, and I had to start climbing on chairs to get things out of cupboards.

Despite these massive changes, I didn't have to worry about my parents noticing any odd behaviour in me. I didn't have to try and act young, finding myself naturally slipping into the persona of my physical age with each passing year.

As I got smaller, I also got weaker. There was one less candle on my birthday cake each year, but they got harder to blow out. It wasn't just people that were getting bigger either. Simple, everyday things like cutlery suddenly became unwieldily large and heavy.

My freedom became increasingly curtailed. There was no more seeing the New Year in. I was sent up to bed long before midnight so my parents could either drink in peace or go out, leaving us with a babysitter. Far from protesting against this, I was happy to go to bed early, succumbing to my young body's need for more sleep.

Despite falling back into my childlike state, I hadn't lost my grip on the reality of what was happening to me. Although I was resigned to my fate, it didn't stop the fear from persisting.

Not only was there the unknown horror of childbirth to endure but also all sorts of worries about other things that were going to happen before that. Would I lose all my memories by the time I reached infancy, or retain some inkling of what was going on?

What about my body? Would I find at two years old that I was now incontinent and back in nappies? The thought of that disgusted me. What about my language and vocabulary? Would I be able to hold a conversation at a year old, or would those abilities go, too?

Whatever happened, it was certainly going to be weird experiencing life as a baby, looking out into the adult world which I had once been a part of. Would I have any understanding by then of what I had been through, or would I have been reduced to a babbling, incomprehensible infant?

I found it difficult to sleep on the night before my seventh birthday, as I was beset by vivid dreams that haunted me with snapshots of the adult life I had left behind, interspersed with visions of what was still to come.

I dreamt of Lily and Phoebe, and the obscene cake they had baked me, the three of us falling about laughing together.

Then, the dream changed as the two of them metamorphosed into my parents, the cake also changing into a cute teddy bear. I was tiny in the dream and sitting in a high chair as my parents stood over me, urging me to blow out the single candle on it with my puny, year-old lungs.

Then I felt a hot and wet feeling between my legs. Looking down, I saw that I was wearing a nappy which I had just filled with urine. It was then that I woke up with a start to discover I hadn't just lost control of my bladder in the dream.

I was seven years old and I had just wet the bed.

I cried then, huge sobs of despair and desperation at the hopelessness of my situation. It was early morning and still dark, but my mother heard me from her room and came in to comfort me.

"It's OK, Amy, it was just a bad dream," she said, in an attempt to soothe me, putting her arms around me as she did so, and not scolding me for wetting the bed.

I wish I could have opened up then and told her everything. This was a much kinder and more loving mother than the alcoholic, wretched mess she would eventually turn into.

Despite my desperation, I did find comfort in her words, even though I knew that it wasn't simply a bad dream. Lily and Phoebe were real, and maybe the memory of my one-year-old self was real, too, dredged up from some long-forgotten archive somewhere in the back of my mind.

Of course, it would be pointless attempting to explain the truth. It was hard enough trying to convince people about time-travelling as an adult. At this age, it would simply be humoured or dismissed as the overactive imagination of a seven-year-old girl. All I could do was meekly accept the comfort on offer as she ran a bath for me and stripped the sodden sheets from my bed.

Despite my unpleasant night, I did my utmost to banish negative thoughts from my mind and enjoy the day, for my family's sake if nothing else. Mum took me, Rachel and Siobhan to the cinema to see *Home Alone 2*. Afterwards, we went to McDonald's for a special birthday tea.

Realising that this might well be the last Happy Meal I would ever have, I made sure I savoured every mouthful. It was just another milestone in a long series of "lasts".

This had been a good birthday and I went to bed feeling more settled than on the previous evening. I knew the next day, I would be back in 1991 as a five-year-old, but there was no point stressing over it. Just as I always had, I would have to take each year as it came.

Then something happened which changed everything.

Chapter Nineteen
1991

When I woke up on New Year's Eve, 1991, I wasn't where I expected to be.

Instead of my Liverpool home, surrounded by my toys and Disney wallpaper, I was in a room that was briefly unfamiliar. It was dark in the room, with just a tiny gap in the curtains letting in a single ray of morning sunlight. It made the dust in the gap sparkle, but it didn't shine much light on my location.

The unexpected nature of my surroundings gave me a brief flash of hope that I might have broken out of the time loop, but a glance down at my body dashed those. I was another year younger, and smaller than ever.

I leapt out of bed with all the energy of a five-year-old and ran over to the door in search of a light switch, fumbling around until I remembered that I was so small now that I had to reach up for light switches.

Once the room was illuminated, I quickly realised where I was. This was not a child's room, but a large room in an old house. The walls were decorated with yellow, floral wallpaper, which even back in 1991 was probably a good decade or two out of date.

The whole front of the room was dominated by a bay window, in front of which stood a large dressing table. The main feature of the table was an old-fashioned, ornate, three-panel mirror, ordained with a brass frame. Scattered around in front were various colourful boxes.

As my memories flooded back I recalled that these contained various trinkets of jewellery, sewing equipment and make-up items. I used to play with all this when I stayed in this room as a child. This was my grandmother's parlour room, as she liked to call it.

We must have been staying over for New Year. I couldn't recall this particular visit, but did remember the regular visits here as a child when we lived in Liverpool. I had stayed in the room several times over the years but it was the first time I had found myself here since I had started time-travelling.

I suppose I should have been used to waking up in different beds by now, having been in so many during my travels, but it was still a surprise, albeit a pleasant one. It meant I would get to see Oxford one last time.

It also meant I would be spoiled rotten by my grandparents who always bought me loads of treats. My recent return to childhood had rekindled my sweet tooth. I no longer had any interest in alcohol or coffee, instead craving a big bag of Pick'n'Mix from Woolworths in Cowley Centre.

Other than the Millennium party, I hadn't had any opportunities to see my grandparents again, as both had died early in the new century. I had always enjoyed my childhood times with them.

My grandfather, like most men of his generation who lived in this area, had worked all his life at one of the car factories that characterised this part of Oxford. I remembered him proudly telling me once how he had been part of the production line that had produced the very first Mini, way back in 1959.

Keen to see him, I raced down the stairs as fast as my five-year-old legs would carry me, slamming into him with delight as he stood pouring out his tea in the kitchen. Such was my exuberance that I almost knocked the tea strainer out of his hand.

"Whoa there, young Amy," he said, looking down at me with his friendly eyes, beneath a smooth, bald head decorated with just a few wisps of remaining grey hair.

As he placed the tea strainer in the sink, I recalled how back in this century, many more people used to make real tea that you had to pour out and strain. My grandmother would have been horrified at the thought of allowing a tea bag in the house. She swore blind that tea bags were not as good. Not being a tea aficionado, I took their word for it.

"Sorry, Gramps," I said. "I'm just pleased to see you!"

"Would you like some Frosties?" he asked.

I certainly did. Rachel was already sitting at the kitchen table eating hers. We weren't allowed Frosties at home – or any sugar-coated cereal, come to that. But I always got what I wanted from my grandparents. I was pretty sure there would also be fish fingers and homemade chips to look forward to for tea, washed down with jelly and ice cream.

The rest of the day passed very much as expected. Gran took Rachel and me into what we had always called Cowley Centre, despite it now having been rebranded as Templars Square.

I got my Pick'n'Mix, in a cup which I filled up with Cola Bottles, Refresher Chews and Dummies. To finish it off, I went for the Smarties, shaking the cup to ensure they all fell down to fill in the gaps. It all tasted impossibly good. I'm not sure if that was down to my youthful sweet tooth, or if it was that sweets had more sugar and E numbers in them in those days.

Whilst I was gorging myself on the sweets, I had a sudden shock when one of my front teeth came clean out, embedding itself in the half-chewed sweet. I showed my gran who smiled and said.

"It looks like the tooth fairy is due a visit tonight."

217

Of course – I had forgotten all about losing my milk teeth. This was all perfectly normal at my current age. There was something else to worry about. Was I going to have to go through teething trouble as a baby, too?

Back at the house, we had tea and then Rachel and I sat down to watch TV for the evening. My parents were not staying with us over New Year. They had remained up in Liverpool. My grandparents weren't strict on bedtimes which meant we could stay up. However, I realised fairly early on in the evening as I began yawning that there was no way my little body was going to stay awake until midnight.

Throughout my life, I've heard people going on about how much better TV was in the old days, but the evening's viewing was pretty tedious by any era's standards, especially considering that it was New Year's Eve.

First, there was some dire showbiz programme, featuring mostly long-dead celebrities I had never heard of. After that, it was *EastEnders*, which had a little nostalgia value as it featured long-departed characters like Pauline and Arthur Fowler.

EastEnders was followed by *A Question of Sport*, something else of little interest to me, though my grandfather loved it and got nearly all the answers right. Then there was some American movie I had never heard of called *Back to School*. By the time that started I was getting tired and the film was barely ten minutes old before I felt my eyelids drooping.

"Do you want me to take you up, Amy?" asked my grandmother. "Big day, tomorrow, remember? It's your birthday! I can't believe you are going to be six. You look so big!"

I didn't feel big and every other day was my birthday these days but I was happy to agree. I was exhausted. She took me up and bathed me which was another odd experience, after so many years of looking after myself. The younger I got, the more things people did for me. I never appreciated it during my childhood the first time around, but now I realised just how much effort went into raising a child.

I was pretty much asleep as soon as I hit the proverbial pillow that night, my youthful body needing increasing amounts of shut-eye with each passing year.

Before I knew it, I was waking to yet another birthday and yet another New Year. But today was going to be different. I didn't know it yet, but I was about to encounter someone I had never expected to see again.

After all the usual present opening and birthday congratulations, Gran took us into the centre of Oxford on the bus. It was mild for early January, nice enough in fact for us to spend plenty of time outside as long as we were wrapped up warm.

Dressed in brightly coloured woolly hats and scarves, we headed down towards the River Thames, close to a pub called The Head of the River. I remember getting drunk there many years later one summer night with Phoebe and Lily. It all seemed like another world now, almost unreal as if it were a fantasy world that I had invented for myself.

I willed myself to keep strong and hold onto those memories. Phoebe and Lily were real, as was the adult life I had once led. I must not allow the person I once was to become lost in this increasingly undeveloped mind and body.

Gran had made us sandwiches, as she always did. She didn't believe in buying them pre-packed from shops. "A waste of money," she used to proclaim. She had lived through times of austerity and by that, I mean real post-war austerity, not the relatively tame 21st-century version.

219

We walked along the river and into Christ Church Meadow, where we sat down on an old felled tree trunk to eat our lunch. Once we had finished, Gran would let us feed our crusts to the many ducks that bobbed serenely along on the River Cherwell.

It was while Rachel and I were throwing morsels of bread to the massing ducks by the bank that I looked up and saw someone I had never expected to see again.

He seemed to have appeared from nowhere, right beside a tree barely ten yards away from me. I may only have met this man once before, but I knew instantly who he was. His image was indelibly imprinted on my mind.

It was Doctor Gardner.

He was looking around sheepishly as if to check that no one had spotted him. Gran and Rachel hadn't – they were too distracted by the ducks – but I had and I knew this could be my one and only hope of salvation. I had to seize this moment and make the most of it right now.

I dropped the few morsels of bread in my hands and ran towards him. He looked startled, no doubt wondering why on earth a six-year-old girl was racing towards him, and turned quickly, starting to walk away in the opposite direction.

"Doctor Gardner, wait!" I yelled.

Behind me, I heard my gran shouting, "Amy, what do you think you're doing?! Come back at once!"

As soon as I said his name, Doctor Gardner stopped and turned back around. I had clearly got his attention. I had to make the most of it. I knew I would not have much time – seconds at the most and would have to pick my words carefully. I couldn't risk him dismissing whatever I said as the fantastical ramblings of a six-year-old child. It was difficult enough getting anyone to take me seriously at this age, as I had already discovered over the past couple of days.

I would also have Gran to contend with, who was now coming after me. She wasn't exactly hot on my heels, as would be expected on her seventy-year-old legs, but she would soon drag me away when she caught up. I had to be concise, give him the facts and then hope for the best.

Doctor Gardner looked down at me as I approached, giving me a chance to get a good look at him. He was exactly as I had last seen him, right down to the backpack and the weird-looking wand. He was the same age, too.

"Listen, we don't have much time," I began in my squeaky, high-pitched voice. "My name is Amy Reynolds. I was a nurse at the John Radcliffe Hospital in January 2025 when you came in and did something that sent me back in time. Now I'm falling backwards through my own life and I need you to do something about it because in less than two weeks I'm going to reach a time before I was born which means I will be dead."

This was as far as I got before Gran, who had now reached us, interceded.

"I'm so sorry," she said to Doctor Gardner, before grabbing hold of me and wheeling me back the other way. As soon as we were a few yards away she began giving me a right scolding, beginning with, "What have you been told about talking to strange men?"

He hadn't been given the chance to reply and I needed to be sure he had understood. My grandmother had grabbed my hand and was frogmarching me away, but I did my utmost to wriggle free.

Managing to loosen her grip and turn back the other way I yelled, "Please, remember what I said."

Briefly, I caught his gaze and, although he said nothing, there was a flash of recognition in his eyes and a barely perceptible nod of acknowledgement. Meanwhile, my defiance was making Gran even more cross.

"Come away, Amy," she said. "I don't know what's got into you, but we're going home right now. Just you wait until I tell your parents about this."

She glanced over to where my sister was standing, still surrounded by hungry ducks, observing my bizarre behaviour from afar. "Come on, Rachel!" she called.

Grabbing my hand firmly, Gran pulled me back down the path.

"You idiot, Amy. Why do you have to ruin everything?" complained my sister.

I managed to fire one glance back to where Doctor Gardner had been standing to see that he was now walking swiftly away in the opposite direction. He had understood, hadn't he?

I was in the doghouse for the rest of the day, but I didn't care. My unexpected encounter in the park had given me fresh hope that there might still be some way out of this, and if there was, then it had been so worth it.

When I got to bed, I tried to think things over as best as my immature mind would allow. I could no longer analyse things as logically as I had when I was an adult. Clearly, there were areas of my brain now simply no longer physically developed for the task. I became slightly frustrated as I tried to arrange my jumbled thoughts into some sort of order. No wonder kids had so many tantrums.

I knew without doubt that it had been him and that he must have time-travelled to get here. But his journey must have been by other means, as he didn't look any younger than he had that day in the hospital, despite it now being thirty-three years in the past.

He still had that strange device with him, which I was pretty sure was what he must use to travel through time. That would suggest he had at least some element of control over what he was doing, unlike me.

If so, why hadn't he come back to help me before? How could he have let me go through all I had over the past two months when he could have come to rescue me straight away?

Admittedly, much of my adventure had been fun. It had given me opportunities to relive some great and some not-so-great moments of my life. It had also allowed me to see old family and friends I thought had gone forever. Then there was saving Rachel, of course.

Despite all of that, it had still been a frightening experience, largely because of the impending death sentence that had been hanging over my head the whole time.

Now that I had contacted him, would he do anything about it? Could he, even? Many hours had passed since our encounter in the park and there was no sign of him. If he was going to whisk me back to my own time, would he not have come to do it by now? If he could time-travel, then he could have returned at any time during the day to rescue me.

I had assumed that he would be able to find me, but I was beginning to have doubts about that. I hadn't given him my address or anything else other than my name. I was a Reynolds, but these were my maternal grandparents I was staying with and their surname was Spencer. That didn't help. But I couldn't give him any more details because of Gran snatching me away.

I couldn't blame her for that. Ever since the Moors murders, there had been a growing fear of child killers and paedophiles, and any strange man talking to a child in a park would be viewed with suspicion. It was the way the world was going now and would get far worse in the next century as all manner of past abuse cases came to light.

Thinking about all this was exhausting and I felt sleep coming to claim me. Just before I fell asleep I offered up one final prayer that something good might come out of what had taken place today.

Chapter Twenty
2025

I knew almost instantly that I was back. As soon as I opened my eyes, I noticed three things simultaneously.

Firstly, the curtains were open and it was broad daylight outside. I could see right away that I was back in my room in the flat I shared with Lily and Phoebe.

Secondly, my body felt different and I quickly looked down to check. The first things I saw were my breasts, back in place, full, rounded and not quite as firm as they had been at my peak. They were exactly as they had been on the day I had left in my thirty-nine-year-old body.

Finally, there was a familiar-looking man sitting on the end of the bed looking at me.

I sat up, pulling the quilt up around me, the way actresses do in films. I was acutely aware that I was naked.

"Better now?" he asked.

Although I had recognised him straight away I couldn't help noticing that he looked older than when I had last seen him.

"Doctor Gardner?" I inquired.

"Call me, Josh," he replied. "And as I think we may have established before, I'm not actually a doctor."

"Well, Josh," I began. "I hope you've got a bloody good explanation for all of this. One that's good enough to justify sneaking into a naked woman's bedroom uninvited!"

He grinned and said, "Well, it might take a while, and you've got to be at work in two hours, but yeah, I'll give it a shot. I imagine you've got a lot of questions."

"Haven't I just," I replied. "You can start by telling me what took you so long."

"Yes, I'm sorry about that. It's taken an enormously long time to sort out the mess I created that day in the hospital. A large part of that was figuring out how to get your mind back into your proper body at the proper time. It's taken me years."

"Well, I suppose I should be grateful," I replied. "Though to be fair, this was your fault in the first place. It's only right you should sort it out."

"That's alright, I enjoy the challenge of trying to solve these problems," he replied. "Alice, that's my wife, was trying to get me to give up all this time-travelling stuff. Knowing that you needed rescuing gave me a legitimate reason to continue my experiments."

"I guess I should say thank you for coming to rescue me," I said. "How did you find me anyway?"

"Well, this helped," he said, producing a faded and crumpled letter from his pocket and handing it to me.

"It's the letter I wrote to Professor Hamilton!" I exclaimed. "So you know him? Why didn't he reply?"

"He was my mentor at the university," replied Josh. "He did receive your letter but didn't do anything with it. He couldn't do anything with it because he never discovered how to time-travel. It ended up filed away with all his other correspondence. He didn't make the connection to me, despite you referring to me as Doctor Gardner, because I hadn't started working with him then. I was also in my early twenties, not fifty, as you stated in the letter."

"That's time travel for you," I replied. "People aren't always the age you expect them to be."

"Indeed," replied Josh. "After you called me Doctor Gardner in the park, it struck a bell because I remembered him

226

mentioning your name years and years ago in one of our many conversations about time travel. Yours was one of many letters he had received, all of which he had concluded were from fakers. I realised after you approached me in the park that your letter must have been genuine. As soon as I got the chance I went back through his files and retrieved it."

"And I thought writing that letter had been a waste of time," I replied.

"It's a good job you did," said Josh. "It made tracking you down a lot easier. I was able to track your family history and eventually trace you to your grandparents' home in 1992. It was very fortunate you ran into me when you did. As luck would have it, I spent several months in Oxford in 1992. But that's another story."

"Well I'm pleased my letter wasn't written in vain," I replied. "Now, perhaps you ought to explain how all this happened in the first place."

"I'll do my best," he said. "But it's quite complicated."

"Just give me the edited highlights," I replied. "You don't need to go into the technicalities."

"OK, well, in a nutshell, I was doing research into the existence of parallel universes and traced the origin of many of them to a specific point in the past. That was 2025 in the hospital room where we met."

"So you're from my future?" I asked.

"Yes, many decades in the future," he replied. "When that all happened, I had come from 2055. But even that was a few years ago for me now."

"Wow!" I replied. "Is it all flying cars and teleporting by then?" I asked.

"Not really," he replied. "But we do have a lot of robots. Anyway that night in the hospital, both myself and another

227

version of myself from a different universe attempted to open the time vortex at the same time. It caused a massive feedback loop which transported you, me, and the dead man on the bed back through time in three different ways."

"So Thomas Scott went back through time, too? Have you brought him back to the present day, too?"

"Unfortunately not," replied Josh. "There would be no point, as he had already died."

"So what happened to him?" I asked.

"He travelled back in time just as you did, but on a much slower trajectory. He lived his entire life day by day in reverse, all the way back to the day he was born."

"Then what happened?" I asked.

"The only thing I could do was reverse the effect, transplanting his mind into a newborn body in a separate universe moving forward. Effectively he gets to start his life again from scratch."

"So you can do that?" I asked. "Transfer consciousness between bodies?"

"That's what I've been working on these past fifteen years. And not just me, come to that. The whole scientific community has been working towards uploading brains to robot bodies so that we can all now live forever."

"Is that how you got me back to the present day?" I asked.

"Yes. I've managed to adapt my time travel technology to allow people to visit their own past by transferring their consciousness into their former bodies. This is effectively what was happening to you, but spontaneously in your case. I just whisked your mind out of your 1992 body and into this one."

"And what happened to you?" I asked. "You said the accident sent you back in time, too."

"It wasn't just back in time in my case," replied Josh. "I was shifting between different universes as well. It wasn't just my mind, but my body, too. That's why I didn't look younger when you saw me in the park."

"But you got back eventually?" I asked. "You wouldn't be here otherwise."

"Eventually, but it was a long and tortuous process. I've seen things in other worlds you could scarcely imagine. And as for my six months in 1992, they weren't straightforward by any means!"

Remembering Gary and all the other things that happened, I knew what my next question would have to be.

"So what about all the stuff I did back in the past? Someone ended up dead because of me. Did you know that? Is he still dead?"

"There's nothing to worry about," he replied. "Everything here is exactly as it was when you left. That's the thing about time travel. Every time you travel back in time you create a new universe with a new timeline. So as far as your life here is concerned, nothing's changed."

"Gary's still alive?" I asked.

"He is," replied Josh.

"And Rachel?" I said, already fearing the answer.

"As I said, everything here is as it was."

"So all that effort I went to to save her was for nothing?" I said despairingly.

"Not at all," he replied. "There are several other universes in existence now where she is alive and well, thanks to your warning about the tsunami."

"But I can't see her?"

"No," he confirmed. "But isn't it enough to know that she's out there somewhere in another universe, alive and kicking – thanks to you?"

He was right. I was no worse off than I had been before all this started and this was some consolation.

"Have you seen everything I've done?" I asked, feeling naked not just in my body but also in my mind. How much did he know? If he could transfer my mind from one body to another, could he peer at my innermost thoughts, too?

"Relax, I've only seen the edited highlights," he said, grinning. "Your secrets are safe with me. I must say those stunts you pulled on your ex were pretty entertaining. The incident with the vegetable knife was unfortunate, admittedly, but who could have foreseen that?"

"Does that mean that I'm in jail in the world where that happened? I got hauled in by the police, you know."

"Would it make you feel better if I told you that you got off scot-free?" asked Josh. "Or, even better, that Rob went down for manslaughter?"

"Yes, it would," I replied, and it did make me feel better. Even if I had engineered the whole situation, none of it would have happened if he hadn't been messing around with that bitch next door.

"All's well that ends well, then," I added. "Is that it, then?"

"There's just one more thing," said Josh. "I've brought you back to the afternoon before the accident. You need to go into work and do everything as you did before with one notable exception. When the time comes to prepare Thomas's body to be taken down, stay clear of the room until 3.30am. Make sure Carmen stays away, too. I'll be in there cleaning up."

"Cleaning up?" I inquired.

"Yes – putting right what went wrong before. In fact, I've already done it, but you need to stay out of the way just so we don't open up any more confusing timelines."

"Then what – you go back to the future to live happily ever after?"

"You know, I really do hope so this time," said Josh. "I seem to spend most of my time these days putting right problems in the timeline. As soon as I fix one thing, something else goes wrong. It's like patching a hole in a bucket which immediately then springs two new leaks. It's an incredibly complex system what with all these universes popping into existence here, there and everywhere. But someone's got to look after it."

"Sounds to me like you're the cause of half these problems," I replied. "Take that debacle in the hospital for a start. That wouldn't have happened if you hadn't been tinkering about with time."

"You're not wrong," replied Josh. "Sometimes I wish I'd never started all this, but I guess it's my raison d'être now. Still, at least I've always tried to use time travel for good reasons."

"And what if someone else out there had less pure motives? You can't be the only time traveller in existence, surely?"

"It's funny you should say that," he began. "But that's yet another story. Right now all you need to know is that your world is safe. All you need to do is get on with your life like before."

"Speaking of which, I need to get up and get dressed," I said. "So if you wouldn't mind…?" I gestured towards the door.

231

"No need for a door," he said, reaching into his backpack and pulling out a familiar-looking object. "I've got this."

"Well, you just be careful where you point that thing!" I exclaimed. "Remember what happened last time!"

"That's what she said," he replied, laughing and eliciting a small chuckle from me, too. Strangely, I was going to miss this mysterious time-travelling man.

"Will I ever see you again?" I asked.

"Do you want to?" he replied.

Did I want to? It was an interesting question. Despite the relief of being back where I belonged, part of me was going to miss the excitement that my time travelling had brought, even if I had spent most of it worrying that I was about to die.

"Tell you what," I said. "How about I become your special agent in this time zone? If you ever find yourself back in this time and need someone with time-travel experience to help you on one of your projects, then look me up."

"I'll do that," he said. "And now, I must go."

He held out his device in front of him which I noticed wasn't the same as the one he had had in the past. This looked newer, made from a shinier metal of a type I didn't recognise. It was also larger with more buttons on the front than I remembered.

"An upgrade?" I asked.

"Yes, and it does a lot more than the old one did. And this one actually works properly," he said. "Well, I guess this is it."

He pressed a button and began to step forward.

"Until next time," I said and watched as he disappeared. For a few seconds I held the quilt close to me, as if, irrationally, I believed he could still see me before I let it drop and began to look for some clothes.

As I did so, I heard the telltale clink of coffee mugs from out in the flat.

Phoebe and Lily! I felt overwhelmed with joy at the thought of seeing them again. Pulling on just a T-shirt and knickers, not caring if this would offend Lily, I wrenched the door handle open and ran out into the kitchen.

There they were, standing by the coffee machine, cups in hand, the picture of normality. If they were surprised at my sudden appearance, they were even more taken aback when I launched myself around the pair of them in a huge group hug, almost knocking their cups out of their hands in the process.

They must have thought I was crazy, but I didn't care because right now I was exactly where I belonged, with the two people I loved more than anyone else alive in the world.

The End…for now - but the story continues in *Return to Tomorrow.*

The Time Bubble Collection

The Time Bubble is the first in an epic series of adventures. To find out more, please head over to my author page on Amazon where you can find them individually, or in box sets:

UK: https://www.amazon.co.uk/Jason-Ayres/e/B00CQO4XJC/

US: https://www.amazon.com/Jason-Ayres/e/B00CQO4XJC/

Return to Tomorrow

If you knew the future, would you preserve the timeline, or rewrite history?

Thomas Scott has already lived his life twice before. At night he dreams about future events, determined not to change anything so that he can meet his wife-to-be in the right place at the right time.

Everything is going according to plan until another time traveller arrives from the future with other ideas.

Ben Lewis, given a second chance in his eighteen-year-old body to put right a life he squandered the first time around, plans to exploit his knowledge of the future for his own ends. When their paths cross in Oxford in 1988, a clash ensues, with Thomas attempting to prevent Ben from disrupting the timeline, and Ben revelling in the doing the exact opposite.

A decade later, the stage is set for a final showdown amidst the blazing heat of Ibiza, during the peak of the 1990s clubbing scene. Can Thomas preserve the fabric of time, or will Ben corrupt it beyond repair?

UK: https://www.amazon.co.uk/gp/product/B08VMRMVC1
US: https://www.amazon.com/gp/product/B08VMRMVC1

A Year in the Life Series

Revisit the 1980s alongside an array of colourful characters as they travel back forty years in time, each getting to live a calendar year of their life over again.

Armed with only a mysterious bracelet to guide them, passed on from person to person, each traveller in time becomes the custodian of the timeline. Their mission is to keep the timeline on track or to steer it back on course where required.

Whether it's in the wider world - preventing a crime, saving a life, or making changes in their own lives to secure a better future, it all takes place against a rich backdrop of the music, news, and culture of that most memorable of decades - the 1980s!

1) 1980: A Year in the Life of Keith Diamond
2) 1981: A Year in the Life of Nick Taylor
3) 1982: A Year in the Life of Wendy Wood

UK: https://www.amazon.co.uk/dp/B0CLKVM4H9
US: https://www.amazon.com/dp/B0CLKVM4H9

1980: A Year in the Life of Keith Diamond

Relive the 1980s in this rip-roaring time travel adventure from bestselling author, Jason Ayres.

As the 2020s dawn, Keith Diamond, the self-styled 'Diamond Geezer', works as a shock jock presenter at controversial radio station, ChatFM. When the station comes under new management, Keith finds himself surplus to requirements. His employment prospects look bleak until a stranger gives him a bracelet that catapults him forty years back in time to when he was a young journalist. Soaking up the culture, Keith immerses himself in the music scene, going to see legendary bands like The Clash, Blondie, and The Specials, but soon there are more important tasks at hand.

Working in Fleet Street, Keith finds himself thrust into the news stories of the day. These range from the hunt for the Yorkshire Ripper to the death of John Lennon, plus the world's obsession with "Who Shot JR?" From a personal perspective, 1980 is a pivotal year on which both his and many of his friends' destinies depend. Can he rectify past mistakes, avert disasters, and reshape both his future and that of others?

Join Keith, as he revisits the culture and events of 1980, in this humorous and thought-provoking time travel story.

UK: https://www.amazon.co.uk/gp/product/B0CN3VY6TJ/
US: https://www.amazon.com/gp/product/B0CN3VY6TJ/

The Ronnie and Bernard Adventures

The Ronnie and Bernard Adventures are a pair of humorous novels with mild science fiction and horror elements set in the 1970s. The stories follow the fortunes of two actors from very different backgrounds.

Together they tackle mysteries, travel in time, and negotiate the rocky path of life as jobbing actors, from daytime soaps to panto.

Anyone who remembers the 1970s will love these nostalgic stories looking back at a time when life was simpler, and the world didn't take itself too seriously. Packed with period detail, humour, and references to the era, they are the perfect antidote to modern living.

1) The Crooked Line
2) The Haunted Theatre

UK: https://www.amazon.co.uk/Jason-Ayres/e/B0BR9SMPPY/
US: https://www.amazon.com/Jason-Ayres/e/B0BR9SMPPY/

The Haunted Theatre

Enjoy a trip back to the British seaside in 1974 in the latest time-travelling adventure from bestselling author, Jason Ayres.

After their long-running soap opera is axed by the network, actors Ronnie and Bernard face differing fortunes in their quest to further their careers. Bernard is much in demand but Ronnie looks washed-up. When the only offer on the table is to be the new Bungle in Rainbow, things are starting to look bleak.

When millionaire holiday camp owner Bobby Burton offers Bernard the starring role in his Christmas panto, he jumps at the chance, bringing Ronnie along for the ride. Together, they travel to the up-and-coming holiday resort of Skegmouth.

After a weekend of mishaps and misunderstandings, largely due to Ronnie's indiscretions, the pair finally make it to The Grand Theatre on the end of the pier. Rumours abound about the strange nature of the theatre, in particular regarding the mysterious disappearance of a music hall star in 1906.

Ronnie and Bernard soon discover that the theatre is indeed not what it seems when they become trapped in time, with seemingly no means of escape.

UK: https://www.amazon.co.uk/gp/product/B0BRY84XFD
US: https://www.amazon.com/gp/product/B0BRY84XFD

Follow the Author

To ensure you never miss a release, or to be informed of special deals on Amazon, sign up to follow me on my author page which can be found here:

https://www.amazon.co.uk/stores/Jason-Ayres/author/B00CQO4XJC

For exclusive content from me, quarterly newsletters and occasional freebies and offers, sign up to my mailing list here:

https://www.jasonayres.co.uk/contact/ or email me directly: jason.ayres@btinternet.com

And of course, there is Facebook, X, and YouTube!

https://www.facebook.com/TheTimeBubble/

https://twitter.com/TheTimeBubble/

https://www.youtube.com/channel/UCg13jmfTUTFCqWWZrPmXqJQ

Finally, if you loved this book and have the time to leave a star rating or review on Amazon, it is always hugely appreciated!

Printed in Great Britain
by Amazon

55165674R00142